Acclaim for *Christmas*
by Phyllis Clark Nichols

"This charming tale will sharpen your appetite for the true spirit of Christmas!"
—Debbie Macomber, #1 *New York Times* Bestselling Author

Christmas at Grey Sage by Phyllis Clark Nichols is a heartwarming, comical frolic from the first page. I fell in love with Maude and Silas and the Unlikely Christmas Party entourage. Forced to stay together at the Grey Sage Inn in New Mexico one snowy Christmas, a band of eclectic travelers trying to escape Christmas find the joy and peace of the season once again and help inn-owners Maude and Silas heal from a long-ago tragedy.

This book is what Christmas is all about. I didn't want to leave the inn. But the recipes included at the end of this story will make me feel as if I'm there once again, sitting by the fire on a snowy night. Curl up with some hot chocolate and enjoy your stay at the Grey Sage Inn. You will have a blast!
—Lenora Worth, *NY Times*, *USA Today* and *PW* Bestselling Author

Christmas at Grey Sage is a beautifully gentle story about grief, friendship, and the unlikely companionship of strangers that will leave you smiling and singing carols as you close its pages. Phyllis Nichols has a knack of creating an enchanting storyworld, populated by diverse and quirky characters you can't help but root for. A satisfying and fun holiday read.
—Mary DeMuth, author of over 30 books, including *The Muir House*

Phyllis Clark Nichols has done it once more! In this new book, she deals again, masterfully, with the topic of Christmas. In an accessible but deep way, her narrative connects the readers with a collective human wealth of experiences, feelings, senses, symbols, and relationships, inviting them to reflect on their own wounds, in order to emerge with a new sense of joy and hope, not only for Christmas, but for life.
—Nora O. Lozano, PhD
Executive Director, Latina Leadership Institute
Professor of Theological Studies, Baptist University of the Américas

Silent Days, Holy Night

Phyllis Clark Nichols

GILEAD PUBLISHING

Published by Gilead Publishing, LLC,
Wheaton, Illinois, USA.
www.gileadpublishing.com

ISBN: 978-1-68370-149-1 (printed softcover)
ISBN: 978-1-68370-150-7 (ebook)

Cover design by thedugandesigngroup.com
Interior design by Jennifer Crosswhite, Tandem Services
Ebook production by Book Genesis, Inc.

Printed in the United States of America.
18 19 20 21 22 23 24 / 5 4 3 2 1

For Janie J, my gentle friend who always has been there with an encouraging word

Prologue

D ON'T TELL ME. YOU'RE WHAT?" I hit the brake, and the car skids a bit but stays on the ice-covered lane before coming to a stop. "But, Piper, you are coming, aren't you? For the Christmas opening, I mean?"

"Well, I … and …" Her voice crackles and then trails off midsentence.

"Piper! Piper? Can you hear me?" I wait. *Oh, rats! No signal. I'll call her back on the landline when I get there. Just a few more turns, then I'll be at the top. What a scene!*

I put the Jeep in park and grab my phone. *If someone comes up the lane, sorry. Better hold on to this moment. Moments come and go quickly. This just might be next year's Christmas card from Emerald Crest.*

The melting ice drips from the naked limbs of the beech trees, but the boughs of the white pines still nestle last night's snow. The powder dusts my shoulder when I brush a pine limb, so I step into the ruts away from the trees and walk up the lane about ten yards for the very best shot.

There. The image. "Emerald Crest, enthroned on a

snow-covered peak like a beryl palace against a cloudless blue topaz sky." Those are the words of the advertising executive who just finished printing our winter brochures. Perfect description of this morning.

I trudge through the ruts up the hill to the west to get Red Spruce Knob in the background. It wears a fresh white blanket this morning. *Thank you, Father, for providing that early morning sun like a spotlight on that old mansion. Click. Click. Got it. This moment may never come again, but I can hang on to it now.*

I head back to the vehicle, grateful for my front-row seat to this December morning's scene peeking through these trees. West Virginia has welcomed me back home in fine fashion. College in Fort Worth, Texas, behind me and my dream job ahead of me. Oh, these hills and trees ... Ah, trees. They call anything that grows above twelve feet tall a tree in Texas because they've never seen the chestnuts and maples and beech trees in West Virginia. And color? A cactus is green until it turns brown and dies. But the colors of leaves on sycamore trees? I have a new I've-been-away-from-home appreciation for them, scaly bark and all.

I slog back down the hill, brush the snow off my shoulder, and climb back into the driver's seat. Another couple of hairpin turns, and I am in the driveway. In front of me, Mrs. Finch, red stilettos firmly planted on the front sidewalk, points to the stone chimney, and Mr. Hornsby watches the snow he's kicking with his pointed-toed boot. His chin is practically on his chest, and his head moves from side to side. I gather they are having another one of their discussions.

I park and get out of the Jeep. "Good morning, Mrs. Finch and Mr. Hornsby."

She looks at her watch. "It's about time. Now that you're here, maybe Edgar will get to work and do what he's told."

Mr. Hornsby never looks up. "Julia's on time whenever she gets here. We're both at work, but I'm not a-goin' to do that, not that thing."

I've seen Mr. Hornsby with his hands in his pockets before,

and this has nothing to do with subfreezing temperatures. It has everything to do with being resolute. "So, tell me, Mr. Hornsby, what is it that you're not going to do this morning?"

"Mrs. Finch here wants me to pull down all these ivy vines from the chimney, and I'm not a-doin' that this mornin'—or any mornin', for that matter. Mrs. Lafferty planted this ivy decades ago, before either of you were born, and I'm not a-pullin' it down."

Mrs. Finch's hands are on her hips.

Not the first time I've seen her like this. "So, Mrs. Finch, why is it you want the vines pulled down?"

"What do you mean why? Don't you have eyes? Look at it." She steps closer to the chimney and breaks off a twig. "It's gnarly and dead, and it really looks deader than it is. Besides, I have ideas about something spectacular to do with this chimney. Something that would dazzle our guests when they drive up to the mansion."

Mr. Hornsby stops kicking snow and shaking his head, his hands still in his pockets. "If I pull the vines down, the chimney's bare forever. So, do you have something spectacular in mind for next spring when the ivy would be turnin' green and coverin' this stone chimney? These vines are only bare for about four months, and even then they're saying somethin'. Even in the winter, they're a livin' part of Emerald Crest, and I'm not a-removin' them."

My dream job? For the last two weeks, I've done little more than referee the competition between these obstinate two. Our opening is in two days, I remind myself. *All this will be over, and my real job begins.* "I love that you have spectacular decorating ideas, Mrs. Finch, and I know that you have envisioned such beautiful things for our gala." I cross my gloved fingers behind my back. *Jesus, forgive me for that fib. I'm just trying to keep peace here.* I know that most of her visions and spectacular ideas come from magazines she purchases down at the drugstore.

"And … Mr. Hornsby, I'm so happy to hear that you revere Emerald Crest's history. And it would be a bit sad to see the ivy go. Maybe the solution here is to ask Mr. Lafferty what his preference would be." *Mr. Hornsby and I can always play the Mr. Lafferty card. Henrietta Finch can't.*

Mrs. Finch heads to the front door in one of her snits, mumbling as she goes. "Well, I would have already asked him if I could."

Diplomatically, I wait until she disappears inside. "Mr. Hornsby, I think we've taken care of that issue. So, since I don't think you'll be pulling down ivy vines this morning, would you mind helping me unload these packages and get them inside?"

Mr. Hornsby is grinning on the inside, and it sneaks out one side of his mouth. He removes his hands from his pockets and grabs a couple of boxes. "Why, I'd just be happy to, Julia. Thank you for rescuin' me and the ivy vines this mornin'. And for saving the vireos. They like nestin' in the ivy in the spring."

I follow behind him with three bags of tinsel, ribbon, and red Christmas balls. "Just so you know, Mr. Hornsby, I'm not planning to involve Mr. Lafferty in this discussion. We both know what he'd say. I think hanging the sparkling lights in the pines lining the driveway is on this morning's list. But that was before we got snow. The ice is melting from the tree limbs, and we don't want you getting electrified this morning. You know that thing about electricity and water. Maybe it'll warm up and be dry by afternoon. You might want to find something to do out of hearing distance of Mrs. Finch in the meantime, though." We step through the front door into the foyer.

"Then I think I'll split some firewood out behind the shed. Henrietta Finch won't come lookin' for me out there. She wouldn't like gettin' mud on her red, high-heeled shoes. Where would you like these boxes?"

"Just put them on the counter in the butler's pantry. They're punch cups, and Mrs. Finch likes things out of sight, you know."

Mr. Hornsby puts the boxes on the counter and steadies them. "And I'll be out of her sight for sure. If you'd rather help me split wood than split hairs with Henrietta, you know where I'll be."

"I just might take you up on that. I'm not wearing red, high-heeled shoes. Thanks for your help." I stuff the three bags beside the two boxes on the counter, reach inside my purse for my cell phone, and dial Piper's number. She answers right away.

"Julia! What happened to you?"

"No, no, I'm fine, Piper. Sorry I frightened you. Signal is spotty out here. Just tell me, will you be here?" I'm prepared to beg, bribe, or belittle to get her here.

"I'm coming, Julia. Wouldn't miss it. I have a show tonight, so Mom and I will fly into Bridgeport tomorrow and rent a car."

"I'll come and get you."

"No need. You have too much to do, and besides, we'd like to have a car." She pauses. "Shoot. Gotta go—rehearsal. See you late tomorrow."

"Oh yes! You made my day, my Christmas, my year, maybe my whole life. This just wouldn't be the same if you weren't here. Later."

I disconnect and stare at my phone with a huge smile. She's coming. Piper—the sister I never had. I remember growing up together, making footprints around this place, and I could not imagine celebrating without her.

I nearly bump into Mrs. Schumacher on my way into the kitchen. "Oh, I'm so sorry. I should be more careful. We seem to be moving around here like bees to a hive lately. I'm sure you're not used to that."

"Yes, we are. Moving around, I mean. And no, I'm not used to it, but I guess I need to get used to it." She smooths her apron and checks to see if she spilled any of the tea out of the cup she carries. "Hot cinnamon-raisin scones with orange butter are on the counter, and I just made a fresh pot of coffee."

"Sounds perfect for a morning like this one. How is Mr. Lafferty? I do hope he's feeling better."

"Yes, he's much better. Still in his room, though, and I'm not certain he'll be down today. I'm taking him another cup of my warm potion he thinks is tea. That's why he's better, you know. I think he'll be in great shape for the gala. Let's allow him to rest and not bother him with any details today, agreed?"

"Yes, ma'am. Please tell him I'm here, and I'm counting on him. Did he finish it yet?"

"Not quite. He said it still needs work. But you know how he is: never satisfied. There is always just a bit of something else he thinks he should do." She heads toward the stairs.

"I know it will be spectacular. I'll find Mrs. Finch and offer her a warm scone. Hopefully it'll sweeten her disposition. Oh, and I just spoke with Piper. She *will* be here for the gala. I was beginning to think her schedule wouldn't allow it. Please let Mr. Lafferty know."

"Lovely. He'll be so pleased to see her again." Mrs. Schumacher turns around and grins at me. "Oh, and I have another special tea for Henrietta's disposition if you'd like me to brew it."

I wink at her and then sit at the breakfast table with my calendar and a warm scone. Normally I would have reached for the apricot preserves, but Mrs. Schumacher's orange butter is better on this cold morning. I look down my list for today and review the plan for the next couple of days. It's all coming together finally—food, decorations, speaker, and entertainment, and the RSVP list is growing each day. Now, if Mr. Lafferty could just finish it, then everything would be perfect.

Rumbles from the garden room sound like Mrs. Finch is rearranging furniture. That's not happening even if it means one of Mrs. Schumacher's special cups of tea. I sip the last drop of my coffee, which also has a sprinkle of cinnamon in it, and put a warm scone on a plate as a peace offering for what might come out of my mouth.

The garden room is my favorite room in the house. It's more like a loggia connecting two wings of the mansion. The exterior green granite wall rises from the green marble floor for about three feet. Then the stone becomes the stage for paned glass that rises to a twenty-foot ceiling. Every lead pane sparkles despite the aberrations that hint at its age. And every sill, casing, sash, and muntin are painted a glossy white. It has been like that since the house was built decades ago.

Beyond those panes are magnificent, manicured gardens. In the spring and summer, smooth brick paths snaking through raised beds of herbs and flowers and trimmed hedges and boxwoods make it feel like a maze. Then there are the fruit trees carefully planted for sun and shade. The limbs are bare now, but they'll be fruit-filled boughs for nesting birds come April.

Mr. Hornsby is right. Even in the winter, there is beauty in bare branches, especially these that allow glimpses into the distant mountains.

And then there is the garden art, mostly made of concrete and natural stone. I know every piece. Grancie is right in saying Mrs. Lafferty had an affinity for all things beautiful, and she must have had an affinity for statues of playful children and animals. They only peek through the garden when it's in bloom, but they are in full sight in December.

The real garden is through the window, but framed garden prints and oil paintings of flowers and birds give the appearance of another garden on the back wall of this room. All through the space are multi-patterned, chintz-covered sofas and chairs. Mrs. Lafferty might have been Irish, but this garden room is as English as it gets. Every piece of furniture here hugs me, and there is always a table nearby where I can set my cup of tea or my glass of lemonade.

But the most comfortable seat in the room for me is the piano bench. That Steinway rosewood grand takes center stage in front of the paned windows looking out on all of West Virginia. Mrs. Lafferty's needlepoint cushion is still there—another picture of how much she loved birds and flowers. This room is one of my growing-up places—sitting on the piano bench playing for Mr. Lafferty and learning about patience and perseverance in the garden.

I enter the garden room from the door to the kitchen wing. Mrs. Finch steps cautiously back from the piano to admire her work. I barely muffle my gasp.

The piano lid is lowered, and there atop the piano is a heavy drape of green velvet trimmed in gold braid. She steps forward and adjusts the folds in the fabric as it cascades almost to the floor. I don't want to believe what I'm seeing: atop the velvet drape is a sterling-silver candelabra with several arms holding twelve-inch red tapered candles. Silk holly leaves with red plastic berries appear to be growing out of the green velvet.

Ghastly.

As I move closer to the piano, wrestling for ways of telling her that decorating the piano would never do, she steps to a nearby table and reaches for a matching candelabra. Before she can put it next to its mate on the velvet drape, I interrupt her.

"Mrs. Finch, no. Just plain no. That will not do." I shock even myself with my bluntness, and shocking myself is a rare occasion. I could not have been less diplomatic, and I am fully aware that Mrs. Finch does not take well to criticism.

Mrs. Finch's face looks like she might have just seen the ghost of the original Mrs. Lafferty drift across the room. Her eyes are blaring and stretch almost to the size of her open mouth, all showing unbelievable surprise. "I beg your pardon, Julia?"

"I'm sorry, Mrs. Finch, but covering the piano and decorating it simply will not do."

She puts the silver piece on the piano, ignoring what I said, and her hands move back to her hips. "I do believe I was the one hired to decorate Emerald Crest for the gala. And I don't believe I was told to take my orders from you, missy. First it was the ivy, and now the piano. Just who do you think you are, Julia Russell?"

"I apologize, Mrs. Finch. What you say is true. And I think the velvet drape and silver candelabras are lovely, and even the fake holly. And I'm certain you'll find a perfect place for it all, but it won't be on the piano."

"Well, it is if I say it is."

"No, ma'am, it is not. I do not mean to be disrespectful, but this piano is not a piece of furniture, and there are things that apparently you do not understand." I set the plate holding the scone down on a chairside table and begin carefully removing the candelabra and the silk greenery.

"One thing I do understand is you're still just as willful as you were when you were ten years old. Your mom and your grandmother would be ashamed if they knew how you were speaking to me."

She doesn't really know Mom or Grancie if that's what she thinks. "No, ma'am, they would not. In fact, I think they'd both be cheering me on and helping me get these decorations moved to where they'll be more appropriate. I'll gladly help you get them to someplace else. Where would you like me to put them?"

"Wherever you like, Miss Russell." Mrs. Finch stomps out of the room, her red heels clicking.

Mrs. Schumacher comes in through the library door just as Mrs. Finch clears the room. Standing still, Mrs. Schumacher allows her eyes to survey the room and settle on me holding two silver candelabras. "Here, let me help you with all that." She picks up the last pieces of greenery and velvet drape. "I suppose we can add this to the list of things Henrietta's unhappy about."

"I suppose we can."

"Need I make my special tea for her?"

"Yes. Several gallons, please. I'd like to give her a bath in it. Why we decided it was best to hire that woman is beyond me."

"Perhaps it might have been easier had you explained the real reason you don't want these things on the piano."

"Perhaps. But I didn't, and I'm glad I didn't give her the scone I brought for her." I pick it up and start eating it myself. When the butter drips down my hand, I lick it right in front of Mrs. Schumacher.

Her voice is soft and gentle. She can still scold me with a question. "You're all grown up now, Julia. Educating people, that's what you're about, isn't it?" She leaves the room before I can answer. Maybe she wants me to think about it. I think she learned that from Mr. Lafferty.

I am alone in the room. I finish my scone and return the candelabras to their box on the sofa. Then I walk to the piano, lift the ebony lid, and secure it in its highest position with the lid prop. I run my fingers over the strings and gaze at the distant mountains, looking like they were frosted with the glaze Mrs. Schumacher puts on her Christmas cookies, and remember. I remember the first time I played this piano sixteen years ago and why the lid is always lifted. And then I remember the Christmas of 2002.

Chapter One

Sixteen years earlier in late September 2002

JULIA, DON'T WASTE YOUR TIME arguing with me. You won't win, and besides, what have you really won if you win an argument, unless it's in the courtroom? You remember that, you hear me?" Dad adjusted his tie and picked up his briefcase.

I planted my feet on that knotty pine floor in the front hall. "But Dad, I could go to Piper's until Mom gets home. I don't want to go out there to that old green house. It'll be boring." I had heard stories about that mansion, and none of them made me want to go there. Grancie said it was a lovely place, but some of the boys at school say the old man that lived there was scary. "I could stay by myself. Nobody will report you for neglecting me. I can just stay here and study. That's not boring. I'm not Jackson, and I know better than to play with matches. I am almost eleven, you know."

"Yes, you will be in ten more months, but what you really are right this minute is exasperating! Get your jacket on. It's getting chilly out there." Dad gave me the look that said I had lost. "Trust me. I promise you, visiting Mr. Lafferty will be anything but boring. Hurry, we have to pick up Mrs. Walker."

"But didn't Mr. Lafferty die?" I looked at my skinny self in the hall-tree mirror and tried to tuck my brown corkscrew curls under the hood Grancie had made for me.

"No. Not this Mr. Lafferty the Second. It was Mr. Lafferty the First who died."

"Wha-at? What happened to just calling him Mr. Whatever Lafferty Junior?" I put on my jacket.

"It's a long and complicated story, and you're not ready for that one. Besides, I don't have time. Let's get going." Dad headed toward the door.

I grabbed my book and my backpack. "But you said we have to pick up Mrs. Walker. Why do we have to pick her up? And tell me why this won't be bo-ring?"

"Julia Russell, with your gift for asking questions, I'm positive you'll be the fourth generation of attorneys in this family." Dad opened the front door just in time for a gust of late-afternoon autumn wind.

I knew he was in a hurry, but I thought I might wear him down. "You may recall, Dad, I didn't arrive here with a brain like some preprogrammed computer you buy for your office—I mean, except for all the autonomic stuff that I never have to think about. We all come wired for that. You know, the stuff like breathing and going to the bathroom and blinking my eyes. But there's so much else I need to learn. So how do you expect me to learn those things if I don't ask questions or maybe read and study, like I could be doing right now?"

"'Autonomic'? Really, Julia. See what I mean? You just asked two more questions before I got the first two answered."

"If you didn't make me go with you, then you wouldn't have to hear my questions, would you?"

"Tell me, oh please tell me, you have a book with you."

"I couldn't be reading a biography of Ludwig van

Beethoven if I didn't have it with me, now could I?" I gave it my best German accent. "I think he was a whole lot of genius and slightly crazy. Did you ever read about him?"

"I tell you, never just a simple 'yes, sir' or 'no, sir' out of your mouth. You even answer questions with another question."

We made it to the car before Dad explained about Mrs. Walker. "Listen to me, Julia. You asked about why I needed Mrs. Walker before I got your Beethoven recital. I need Mrs. Walker because she is a sign-language interpreter."

"You mean like language for someone who's deaf?"

"Yes, that's exactly what I mean."

"Beethoven became deaf. But did you know he was deaf when he wrote his last symphony?"

"Julia. Quiet. There's something else you need to know. We don't have much time. So, just listen and no more questions." Then Dad told me about Mr. Lafferty. "Now, don't stare. He uses a wheelchair, and he's deaf. And he doesn't take to strangers. So just sit quietly and read another chapter about Beethoven." Dad paused. "And for God's sake, don't speak loudly to him."

"You mean to Beethoven? He's dead."

"No, I don't mean Beethoven. We were talking about Mr. Lafferty."

"Yes, but pronouns must have antecedents, and the last antecedent you used would have been Beethoven."

Dad raised his voice. "Just don't speak loudly to him."

"You mean loudly like you're speaking to me? And why would I speak loudly to Mr. Lafferty? He can't hear."

Dad put on brakes for the stoplight and turned to the back seat to look me in the face. "You're right. He can't hear, but some folks think if they speak loudly enough he will hear them. He won't. So just don't do that."

"Why are you meeting with Mr. Lafferty?"

"Because I'm his attorney, and I handle all of his business affairs. I've been doing that for years, just like your grandfather was the attorney for the first Mr. Lafferty."

"Well, if you're his attorney and you've been his attorney for years, why didn't you just learn sign language so you could communicate with him yourself?" I could see Dad's face in the rearview mirror. He wrinkled his brow and his eyes got close together. "Then you wouldn't need Mrs. Walker. Good question, Dad? Better than the others?"

"Just do what I say. Sit quietly and read your book, understand?"

"That's weird. So if I can only stare at my book, and I can't speak, why won't this be boring?"

"First of all, you've never seen anything like this house. Mr. Lafferty's a fascinating man. He's highly intelligent, extremely well read, a talented sculptor, and he has a special gift that maybe you'll get to see if you're really lucky."

"You mean his art?"

"Oh, no. You'll see his sculptures. The place is covered with them and his books, but sculpting's not his most unusual gift."

Dad turned into Mrs. Walker's driveway. "Oh, good, she's ready. Punctual as always." He waved at Mrs. Walker, who stood on her front porch holding on to her scarf like it might fly away.

"Or could it be that you're late and she's been standing there for ten minutes waiting on you?" I really wished I hadn't asked that. "So how will I know if I see this gift he has, and is he … is he like a hoarder? One of those people who doesn't throw anything away?"

"We are only three minutes late, and I repeat myself to make my point: Julia, does anything come out of your mouth that doesn't end in a question mark? No, Mr. Lafferty is not a hoarder. Trust me. You'll know his gift if you're fortunate enough to see it. Now sit quietly until we get there." Dad got out to open the door for Mrs. Walker.

I was quiet for the next few minutes. Mr. Lafferty lived out in the countryside. Folks just passing through on their way to Elkins might never know there was such a house on the big hill on the edge of town, but all the town folks knew about the stone manor. In the summertime, it blended into the trees. But now that the leaves were falling, I could see the house from the road. Dad turned off the highway down a lane that wiggled up the hill. The closer we got, the bigger the house got. It was the biggest I'd ever seen, like a giant green castle plopped down and spread out in all directions. Two stories as tall as the pine trees, and three stories in some places.

Dad parked in the circular driveway out front. He opened the back door for me. "You remember what I said, Julia."

"Yes, sir. No talking, and no questions." I mumbled under my breath, "And no fun."

He walked around the car and opened the door for Mrs. Walker. Dad was just that way. No females were allowed to open doors when he was around. My grandfather was just like him.

I followed him and Mrs. Walker up the green granite steps to the porch. The porch was kind of small for such a big house. I'd never seen green stone like the outside walls of this house. In some places, it was as green as the grass in May, with brown streaks running all through it. All the windows had brown shutters.

I thought it rather strange when Dad rang the doorbell. *How's a deaf man who lives alone supposed to know someone's at the door?* But the minute that buzzer was pressed, lights flickered through all the front windows.

Dad must have known I was about to rupture with a question, so he quickly explained how the flashing lights alerted Mr. Lafferty that he had a guest.

The big wooden door with brass hinges creaked when it opened. Too bad there were no flashing lights on the door to let him know the hinges needed oiling.

And then there he was: Mr. Lafferty, the ogre I'd heard stories about. He looked like an ordinary person to me. He had kind blue eyes that moved around a lot under bushy eyebrows. His hair was gray and wavy and looked like he might have been wearing a hat on it all day. He looked old, but his skin was a pinkish white with no wrinkles. He wore a plaid flannel shirt, and he had a different-colored plaid blanket across his legs. His plaids did not match. And it was a little chilly, but not chilly enough for that blanket inside the house.

Mr. Lafferty greeted us silently from his wheelchair. When he motioned for us all to come in, we followed him through the doorway. Dad stayed behind to close the door and to pinch my earlobe. That was my you-better-behave-like-a-good-Russell-daughter alert.

Dad was right, like he mostly was. I had never seen anything like this house. The front door opened into a foyer larger than our garage. It looked like an inside forest with dark wood paneling on the walls and green marble floors and sculptures of birds on tables all around. The room was so big and so hollow that our footsteps created echoes as we walked.

Mr. Lafferty wheeled himself into the dining room to the end of the longest dining table I had ever seen. Dad and Mrs. Walker sat to his right. I was still standing in the archway, looking at carved birds hanging by golden cords from the chandelier above the table, wooden birds perched on the windowsills, and a giant eagle looking as if he was about to take flight from the pedestal at the opposite end of the room. I couldn't wait to tell my friends at school tomorrow that I'd been to the green mansion and I'd met the troll.

Dad motioned for me to sit. I had to put my backpack down before I could pull the big wooden chair away from the table. Big houses wouldn't look right with dainty chairs. I sat across from Mrs. Walker, but I never opened my book. I watched Mr. Lafferty's hands begin to move, and I listened to Mrs. Walker speak. Then Dad would say something, and Mrs. Walker moved her hands while Mr. Lafferty watched. Then Mr. Lafferty made odd motions with his hands, and Mrs. Walker spoke again.

Dad was right. I was not bored. I studied Mr. Lafferty's hands. They were scarred, probably from his sculpting and carving tools, and his fingers were knotty like a pine branch, but they moved nimbly like Grancie's with her knitting needles. I moved my hands under the table, trying to imitate what he was doing. I was so fascinated with his hands that I wasn't paying much attention to what they were talking about until I heard Dad tell him about a family in town that needed help for some medical reasons. I liked medical stuff. A sick coal miner, I thought. I didn't know sign language, but I didn't need to hear what Mrs. Walker said. The sparkle in Mr. Lafferty's eye and the flutter of his hands already told me that some poor family would get the help they needed.

I behaved and didn't interrupt until I needed to go to the bathroom. I really needed to go, but I didn't know where it was. Dad was on the other side of the table, and that was like being across the whole room. I couldn't just blurt it out, so I walked around to where Dad sat and whispered, and he whispered back that the powder room was underneath the curved staircase across the hall where we had come in.

I only weighed sixty-seven pounds, but the *cloppety-clop* of my shoes sounded more like a rhinoceros. I took them off and tiptoed in my sock feet.

In the hall stood two identical doors, side by side, where Dad had told me to go. A house with a boy's and a girl's bathroom? But I didn't know which one was which. The first brass knob I tried was locked, or at least it wouldn't turn. The next one opened. Good. I did not want to disturb Dad again.

Even the bathroom was tiled in green halfway up the wall from the floor and then painted a lighter green above. Pictures of all kinds of birds lined the walls. The mirror above the sink was about the size of a door. The frame looked like golden tree limbs with green leaves made of stone that looked like Grancie's jade Fu dog. These people had a thing about birds. I washed my hands, opened the door, and heard it needed oiling too.

Mr. Lafferty seemed like a nice man to me, not like the stories I'd heard, and I didn't think he would mind if I looked around just a little. The staircase was curved, and the railing was dark carved wood. Beyond the stairs, I could see into a room with large windows. The sun was almost setting, but I could see the garden. It was unlike any I'd ever seen except in my mom's magazines. Trimmed shrubs and beds of flowers and bird feeders were everywhere. Birds flitted around and fed from mesh bags hanging from tree limbs and wooden feeders on top of posts. There were brick-paved paths in all directions. I figured that made it easier for Mr. Lafferty in his wheelchair.

Then I saw it. The piano—the biggest one I'd ever seen, even bigger than my piano teacher's. I supposed a big house needed a big piano. I sat down and raised the lid and ran my fingers over the keys—not white plastic ones, but real ivory keys. I had only read about pianos with real ivory keys. I imagined some poor elephant's misery so somebody could have a piano like this.

I was already learning my music for our Christmas recital, and I really wanted to try it out on a piano with real ivory keys. Then I could tell Mrs. Hawkins all about it.

Now, Jesus, please forgive me for what I'm about to do, but I may never get this chance again. And I really don't think you'd want me to miss it.

I knew how to use the soft pedal, and since Mr. Lafferty couldn't hear anyway, I didn't think my version of "Silent Night, Holy Night" would get much attention. I was wrong. I knew that my footsteps made noise, but I didn't know that sound traveled through this house like an echo chamber. Before I finished two phrases, Mr. Lafferty had come rolling into that room like a bowling ball on its way to a strike, moving one hand like he was conducting an orchestra and pushing his wheelchair with the other. Mrs. Walker was right beside him, trying to keep up and talking real fast. "Don't stop. Don't stop," she was saying in a shrill voice. "Play it again, please. Play it once again."

By then my dad was right behind me, and my right earlobe was between his thumb and index finger.

24

I didn't know what to do. Mr. Lafferty's face was a picture of pure excitement. I looked up at Dad. His wasn't. But he nodded his head and let go of my ear. I guessed that meant it was okay for me to play. So I did, only this time I didn't use the soft pedal. When I started to play, Mr. Lafferty wheeled himself right into the curve of the piano and touched the ebony wood with his right hand. He closed his eyes, and a smile settled on his face. It was like he went somewhere far away to another time. Every time I stopped playing, he wanted me to play again. I only knew three songs, but he heard them all three times.

I thought it sad that Mr. Lafferty couldn't hear the music, but I was glad he liked whatever he was experiencing that I didn't understand. And I was hoping that his liking it might keep me out of a ton of trouble.

Before we left, Mr. Lafferty invited me back to play the piano for him. For once, I didn't know what to say. All I could do was nod my head. I didn't have language for Mr. Lafferty. Except … my grancie said that smiles, hugs, and music were the universal language. I had already smiled at him, and I'd made music for him, so there was nothing left to do but hug him. So that's what I did. I hugged him. He was like hugging Dad's set of golf clubs, and he didn't hug back. I think I scared him. But he smiled just a little when we were leaving, and he waved goodbye.

I had about a million questions when we got into the car. I thought maybe, since Mrs. Walker knew sign language, she might know a bunch of other stuff about being deaf. When Dad breathed between sentences, I said, "Dad, you said Mr. Lafferty's deaf, but I think he can hear. He heard me playing the piano."

"I heard you playing the piano and alerted Mr. Lafferty that I needed to go and retrieve you, Julia. That's when he took off."

Before Dad could say anything else, Mrs. Walker answered. "Oh, he's deaf all right, but that doesn't mean he can't experience music."

"So, what is music like when you can't hear it?"

"He feels it. He's able to sense vibrations in the same part of the brain that you use for hearing. His experience with the piano today was every bit as real as the sounds your dad and I heard."

"That's something I need to know about—brains and hearing. I'd like to know how all that works. I know about the eardrum and vibrations. Must have something to do with that." Mrs. Walker turned around to look at me in the back seat. "Yes. It does. And how the deaf experience music is something that has been thought about and studied for a long time. It's difficult because of our inability to describe what we experience when what we experience is so basic to us. How do you experience music?"

"Hmm, I hear it."

Mrs. Walker turned back around in her seat. "And if you asked Mr. Lafferty that same question, he'd probably tell you he feels it."

"But I feel music too. I mean, it can make me happy or sad just by the way it sounds. Like today, I think Mr. Lafferty really liked 'Jingle Bells.' I think it made him happy."

"Yes, and just like what you hear stirs your feelings, what he experiences, however he experiences it, stirs his emotions too. I'm thinking this isn't the first time Mr. Lafferty has experienced music."

Dad spoke up. "You're right. His mom and grandmother played the piano beautifully, so I'm told. He must have remembered experiencing them play."

The rest of the way home I was quiet. I mostly thought about what had happened at the green mansion, and I wondered if I might get to go back. And I thought about Beethoven, and how he couldn't hear. But he was different; he had heard the orchestra. He knew how every instrument sounded. But Mr. Lafferty ... I wondered if he had ever experienced anything but the piano.

When we got home, Dad settled in his study while Mom

worked in the kitchen. I went upstairs to do my homework. I could tell Jackson was playing video games when I walked by his room. I studied for a while and then pulled out my book about Beethoven, skimming the pages quickly to see what I could find out about his deafness. Mom called us to the dinner table before I got to that part.

I expected to see my grandparents when I got downstairs. My grancie knew lots of stories about the Laffertys, and she liked to tell stories. All I had to do was ask one question, and there she went, and she didn't have an Off button until she was finished. I knew just the question to get her started. And I knew if I asked Dad that question, I'd get no answers, just a "I don't think you need to know all that right now" kind of response.

I helped Mom with the tea. "Where are G-Pa and Grancie? It's Tuesday night. They always eat with us on Tuesdays."

Mom answered as she put the meatloaf on the table. "Couldn't make it tonight. G-Pa's friend from Richmond is here for a few days."

I sat down at my place. Mashed potatoes and gravy, apple salad, Brussels sprouts, and biscuits. I hated Brussels sprouts. Nobody should eat baby cabbages. "But I like it when they eat with us, and I miss them tonight. Maybe I could go there tomorrow after school and spend some time with Grancie."

Mom looked at me over her reading glasses. "And how will you do that when you have your piano lesson tomorrow?"

"Oh, Brussels sprouts!"

Mom turned around from the sink. "Tell me you didn't say Brussels sprouts like a swear word because you're disappointed."

"Oh, no, ma'am. I just noticed them on the table." *Jesus, forgive me.*

"Um-huh. And I'll be seeing them on your plate shortly, won't I?"

I stammered, "Yes, ma'am, but I'm really not very hungry. I had a big lunch and a snack this afternoon."

Jackson came bumbling down the stairs with his headphones hanging around his neck, trying to act cool just because he was thirteen now. He was into everything that included throwing, kicking, hitting, or bouncing a ball. He slumped at the table, but he might eat my Brussels sprouts if I promised to make his bed in the morning.

Dad told Mom all about our trip to Mr. Lafferty's and how I'd played the piano for him. "I thought I might get fired for bringing my daughter to the meeting when it's not bring-your-daughter-to-work day, especially if she showed signs of being a willful child—and she did."

"But Dad, the keys—the piano keys were real ivory, and I couldn't bear not playing real ivory keys. Besides, I didn't think Mr. Lafferty could hear." I dipped the ladle into the gravy bowl four times. Then I stirred that gravy into my potatoes before Mom could see.

"About your piano playing: Did you think I had lost my hearing?"

"No, sir. But I used the soft pedal."

Jackson piped in. "So, what were you doing plundering through the house in the first place?"

I hoped he choked on his biscuit. "Shut up, Jackson. I had to go to the bathroom. I'd like to see what you would have done in that house. Breakable things and birds everywhere, hand-carved wooden birds. With you around, lots of them would have broken wings. You can't move without tearing something up. Your spasticity level is off the convulsive meter."

Jackson shook his head. "Where do you learn words like that? You should get a life."

Mom interrupted. "She learns from reading, Jackson." She turned to me. "I'm very proud of you for playing for Mr. Lafferty today."

I held my nose and ate two Brussels sprouts. I counted out the English peas too, until I finished dinner and excused myself to finish my homework. At 9:01 I was already in bed with my book on Beethoven when Dad knocked on my door.

"Your Mom's talking to Aunt Jane, so I'm the one tucking

you in tonight." Dad sat down on the edge of my bed. "Time for lights out, my number one daughter."

"I'm sorry if I disappointed you today. I didn't mean to. I just couldn't help myself."

"So your curiosity got the best of you? You might remember what it did to the cat. But everything turned out all right for you. Not so much for the cat. And Mr. Lafferty did seem to enjoy your playing."

"Will you take me back with you when you go to see him? Mr. Lafferty asked me to come and play again."

"We'll see."

"Is Mr. Lafferty's special gift talking with his hands? It surely looked like a gift to me."

"No, that's just his language, one of the ways he communicates. You'll know his special gift when you see it, because you have never, and I mean never, seen anything like it. Maybe next time."

"So that means I get to go back to Emerald Crest?"

"Sounds like it, but you need to remember that you're not to talk about meeting Mr. Lafferty. He's a very private man and doesn't want people knowing anything about his business. We need to respect that. Do you understand?"

"Yes, sir."

Dad prayed with me, kissed me goodnight, and turned off my bedside lamp. As soon as he closed my door, that's when the light came on—the light in my brain. I was going to learn sign language. I wanted to talk with Mr. Lafferty, and I didn't want Mrs. Walker telling him what I was saying. She could teach me how to talk with my hands.

Chapter Two

SINCE I CAN'T GO TO Grancie's today, could I go tomorrow?"
I didn't think Dad was looking, so I took another sugar
cube and stirred it into my tea. I'd never wanted to drink
milk when I was little. But when I was three and Grancie
started having cream tea parties with me, she filled my teacup
with milk and only a spoonful of tea. I drank it. She must have
told Mom how to get me to drink milk, so Mom had made me
tea for breakfast since then. And now that I was ten, sometimes
I could have coffee with my milk too. They didn't know I'd
figured all that out a long time ago.

"Three lumps, really, Julia? I can imagine you're the only
child in your class who drinks hot tea for breakfast. That's usually an acquired taste."

Mom put the basket of toast on the table and came to my
rescue. "Drink your coffee, Ben. Two-thirds of her tea is milk."

"You didn't say if I could go to Grancie's tomorrow. May
I, please?"

"We'll have to see if that works for your grandparents.
Remember, they have a guest." Mom went to the stairs to call

Jackson. She did that every morning. I kept telling her she was training him to ignore his clock. She should just let him be late, walk to school, and have to explain his tardiness to Mr. Simms. I thought after one visit with Mr. Simms, Jackson would pay more attention to his alarm clock.

"Dad, do you think Mrs. Walker could teach me how to talk with my hands?"

"I suppose she could, but you know she teaches over at the college in Elkins. Since you're into questions this morning, maybe you should be asking, 'Dad, what do you think about my learning sign language?'"

Mom sat down at the table. "Julia, sign language? You already have something almost every afternoon, and what about your studies and your homework and piano practice?"

"I could do it. I can do it all." I thought I had more of a chance with Dad. "What do you think about my learning sign language?"

I saw Dad glance at Mom like he was asking permission for what he was about to say. "I actually think that learning sign language might be good for her." He looked straight at Mom. "Yes, I do think it would be good. It would teach her about the value of silence." Then he chuckled, and Mom got her now-why-would-you-think-that look.

Jackson came down the stairs, looking like the rumpled comforter on his unmade bed. I'd heard Mom tell Dad one time that Jackson's hygiene habits would change when he discovered girls. I figured girls were still undiscovered, the way he looked this morning.

"Did you say 'silence'? Julia, silent? That's about as likely to happen as our junior varsity team winning the state championship this year." Jackson plopped his biology book on the table and gulped his glass of milk before he reached for the toast.

"I know how to be silent. Remember, I read in silence, Jackson."

He shoved his book toward me. "Well, here. Why don't

you read this and explain it to me? Have you ever read anything about protozoa?"

"Yes. They're singular-celled organisms that behave like animals. That means they eat and move around and prey on other protozoa. They don't have brains. In fact, they're a lot like you, Jackson."

He shook his head that spent way too much time in a football helmet.

"And they are microorganisms. That means they can only be seen under a microscope. And they can cause disease. Serious disease. They're different than protophyta."

"Enough. I got it. Just be quiet. You know, silent."

I muffled my voice. "Protophyta are singular-celled organisms that are more plantlike." That fact would have impressed his teacher, but he wouldn't get to do that. "So could you please talk to Mrs. Walker, Dad? I really want to study sign language. And could you call Grancie today to see if I can visit her tomorrow?"

Mom turned the African violet around on the table to face the sun coming through the breakfast room window. "I'll call her, Julia, but she could still have company."

"And Mrs. Walker?"

Dad answered, "I'll think about it."

Jackson piped up. "You learned about protozoas, and you didn't take biology. So, why don't you just learn sign language the same way?"

"The plural is protozoans, Jackson." I needed to think about what he said. Once in a while, Jackson said something that made sense. *If Mrs. Walker won't teach me, maybe I'll just teach myself.*

Dad stood from the table. "Leaving for school in five minutes." He turned to Mom. "I'll be in the office all day catching up on paperwork. No courthouse business today."

"Today is my day at home. Maybe we could have lunch here together." Mom started to clear the table. "And Julia, I'll pick you up after school for your piano lesson. Do you have your piano books?"

"Yes, ma'am." I grabbed my jacket from the hall tree and headed toward the door.

I didn't see Piper out front or on the playground, so I headed straight for our classroom. I was dying to tell her about my visit to the green mansion, but she wasn't there. They lived out in the country on the other side of town, and sometimes she was late to school when her father was on call. Piper had been my best friend since forever. Her dad was a doctor, and I got to ask him all the questions I wanted to about medicine. He said when I was a little older I could follow him around the hospital for a whole day to see what doctors really do, and he would even take me to the lab. He told me that following him might help me decide about being a doctor. Piper wanted nothing to do with that, but it sounded interesting to me.

Our parents were friends, and Piper didn't have any brothers or sisters. We could almost pass for sisters, though. Except for the hair. We both had blue eyes, but her hair was long and straight and silky. Mine had started out blonde like hers, but curly, and it was getting darker. Mom said that's what had happened to her hair growing up. Now she was a curly dishwater blonde.

Piper liked dancing and acting, so her mom took her all the way to Elkins for lessons, and she performed in a theater there for Christmas. Me? I liked to play the piano, and I mostly liked to read. I'd tried dance lessons for a while because Piper wanted me to and her mom volunteered to do all the driving, but I wasn't very good at dancing. I had Shirley Temple hair, but not Shirley Temple feet. I was better at the piano, but sometimes I still went to Elkins with Piper just to watch her dance at her lessons. She was really good, and she said she was going to be a professional dancer in New York City.

34

I didn't have it figured out yet what I'd be, but I figured if I kept reading and exploring new things, something would just appear right in front of me. Dad thought I'd be the next attorney in the family, and that was a good possibility. Lawyers had to know a lot of stuff about a lot of stuff, and I liked that part. When I talked to G-Pa about my future, he just reminded me I have seven more years to decide and not to rush it. And Dad said he'd changed his mind three times before he decided to become a lawyer. But no matter what, I knew for certain I wouldn't be dancing on a stage in New York City.

Piper came sliding through the classroom door just before the tardy bell rang. I leaned over to her desk and whispered I had something to tell her that she wouldn't believe. She passed me a note later when Mrs. Hinson had her back turned. *Is it about the fall carnival and the hayride? Did Robby ask you to go? I know you like him, and I think he has a crush on you.*

Piper could tell from the expression on my face that the answer was a big, fat no. She seemed more interested in boys these days, and she didn't seem to mind if they acted dumb. But Robby wasn't dumb. He was smart and kind, not like the other boys in my class.

Finally, the bell rang for our morning break, and we walked down the hall and out to the playground. Piper was pulling at the sleeve of my blouse the whole time we walked. "Julia, what's the big secret? What is it that I won't believe?"

We sat down on the bench under the sycamore tree. "Dad took me to Emerald Crest with him yesterday."

"Emerald Crest?"

"Yeah, you know, the huge green mansion that sits on the mountain outside of town. That's Emerald Crest."

"The one where the troll lives?"

"Yes. That one. Only a troll doesn't live there."

"Did you see him?"

"Yes, and I saw the inside of the house. It's, like, castle big, and it's full of wooden birds that Mr. Lafferty has carved. Everything in that house is either wooden or green."

"Who's Mr. Lafferty?"

"He owns the house, and he lives there by himself. He uses a wheelchair."

Angus and Gary walked up. Angus looked at me. "I was standing behind you and I heard what you said. You didn't go to that house, and you didn't see anybody 'cause you'd be dead if you did. That place is haunted."

"That's not so, and you don't know anything about anything, Angus."

"I know what my brother said. He said there's caves out there with people's bones in 'em—bones of people who went on that property and were never seen again."

Gary stepped out from behind Angus. "Yeah, and my grandpa said there's treasure in them caves 'cause that's where the old man kept his money. He was rich, and now he's dead, but he still haunts that place to protect what he buried in them caves."

Angus added his ignorance. "Yeah, what you saw was a ghost of a dead man."

"He was no ghost."

Gary asked, "How do you know? Did he talk to you?"

"No, he can't talk, and he can't hear. He's deaf."

"Um-huh. He can't talk, and he can't hear because he's a ghost, or else you're just lying."

I wanted to slap them silly. It was too late to slap them stupid. "You're right. I'm lying about all the things I saw at Emerald Crest—the birds Mr. Lafferty's carved, the huge house, and the expensive things in it. And I'm lying about playing the piano for him."

Piper spoke up. "You played the piano for him? I thought you just said he was deaf."

"He is deaf, but he can feel the music."

Gary laughed. "You played the piano for a ghost who can't hear? He probably wished he was deaf."

He and Angus started to walk away. But Angus turned around and said, "You're crazy, Julia, and you'd better stay away from there—lights a-flickerin', dead men's bones, and ghosts."

I was just about to tell them Mr. Lafferty was a very rich man who helped a lot of people in Sycamore Hill, but then I remembered what Dad had said. I wasn't supposed to be talking about Mr. Lafferty's business. I could trust Piper, but Gary and Angus were just trouble looking for a place to misbehave.

Jesus, forgive me, but I need to clean up this mess I made. "Ha, ha! I fooled you, Angus. You were just about to believe what I was telling you about going to that mansion, weren't you? Tricked you. I was just trying out the ghost story I'm writing for my Halloween project. Thanks, you gave me some ideas."

Angus turned around again with a frown on his face. He waved his arm like he was brushing me off. I hoped he was.

Piper tugged on my sleeve again. "Julia. Now I don't know what to believe. Was any of what you said true?"

"Every last word I said is true except that last thing I said about tricking Angus and Gary. I've been to the green mansion. I met Mr. Lafferty, and he's real. He's deaf, and he uses a wheelchair, and I'm not supposed to be talking about him."

"Why aren't you supposed to talk about him?"

"Because Dad is his attorney, and I probably heard things I'm not supposed to know. Sort of like if you heard your dad talking to one of his patients on the phone. We're not supposed to talk about that stuff."

"But you can tell me. I won't tell anyone."

"I've already told you everything except one thing, and I can't tell you that. I don't want Mr. Lafferty to fire Dad. And besides, Mr. Lafferty invited me to come back and play the piano for him again, and Dad said I could. Maybe I could ask if you could go with me next time."

The bell rang. Piper stood up from the bench. "Let's go, and I mean back to class. I'm not sure I want to go out to that green mansion with you."

"Believe me, you do."

Chapter Three

I DIDN'T SLEEP MUCH TUESDAY night. I kept thinking about what Angus and Gary had said and wondered why I'd never heard any of those tales. I knew they weren't true, but I couldn't figure why anybody would make up tales like that about Mr. Lafferty and then why anyone would believe them.

I'd heard too many conversations between Dad and G-Pa when they were talking about a case and how they needed to sift through lots of stories to get down to that one kernel of truth—the one kernel that cracked the case.

I was sifting through what I knew, and there were a couple of kernels of truth in what Angus and Gary had said. The Laffertys had always been rich, and there could be caves on that property. Our whole area of West Virginia had caves. But finding human bones in one? I guessed even that could be true. People did get lost in caves in these parts, and they were never found.

My biggest worry wasn't caves or ghosts or even hidden money. It was whether Angus and Gary believed what I'd said, or if they believed my made-up story about what I said. I hoped they hadn't told anyone else about it. Gossips around this town swarmed like mosquitoes in July. But at least I hadn't said anything about Mr. Lafferty helping the town folks who needed help. *Forgive me, Jesus, and I hope I don't get in trouble and Dad doesn't lose his job.*

I was grumpier than usual at breakfast, and Mom said I looked sleepy. I told her the neighbor's dog had kept me awake. Now, that was not a total fib. Rusty had barked a few times late into the night. I just didn't tell Mom I was already awake.

When I got to school, Piper thought I was extra grumpy too. And when she asked me at lunch to tell her more about my visit to the green mansion, my lips were zipped tight. All I had to do was mention her latest dance costume. Subject changed, and all I heard about was red sequins and white tights. No more talk of the mansion or ghosts or my visit.

I suffered through the day until the final bell rang. I just knew if I could get to Grancie's, I'd learn everything I wanted to know about Emerald Crest and Mr. Henry Lafferty the Second. And something told me that was a lot of learning.

Grancie was at the curb waiting for me, honking her horn like I wouldn't know she was there. I climbed into the front seat.

"Hi, sweetie. Hope you had a good day. Did you teach those teachers of yours something today?"

"Yes, ma'am. I showed them my experiment. We've been studying fossils, but now, since it's autumn, we're studying about why leaves change color. They really liked my project."

Grancie giggled and drove toward her house. "Tell me, did you blow anything up?"

"Not this time. I just showed them how there's red and yellow in a leaf even in the springtime when the leaf is green."

"Sounds impressive. Are you telling me there's red and yellow in a green sycamore leaf in June?"

"It's true, Grancie. You just need a bottle of rubbing alcohol, some hot water, and a coffee filter to prove it. Oh, and you must have leaves. I put a few chopped-up, green sycamore leaves in a jar and covered them with alcohol. Then I covered the jar with aluminum foil and put it in a pan of very hot water. I kept changing out the water to keep it hot. That's important. After about thirty minutes, I took off the foil and put one end of a strip of coffee filter down in the alcohol, sort of like a wick in an oil lamp."

I knew Grancie wasn't that interested in my project. But I hoped it would wear her down and she'd be so tired of my gabbing that she'd talk my ears off about the Laffertys to keep me from talking about science anymore.

"Then after about an hour and a half, as the alcohol evaporates, it brings the bands of color up the paper—red, orange, and yellow. See, it's all about the chlorophyll. That's what makes the leaves so green, and it hides the other colors until autumn. But the chlorophyll starts breaking down in the fall because the weather is cooler and there's less sunlight. And when the chlorophyll breaks down, the leaves turn different colors. I just separated the colors using heat and alcohol. That's basically the process of chromatography." By that time we were in the driveway. "I can tell you lots more about chromatography. Would you like to know more about that?"

Grancie got out of the car and headed toward the back porch. "You know, child, I do hope I'm still around when you're grown up. I have a feeling you're going to turn the world upside down, and I'd certainly like to see it. What do you say we go inside? I have some tasty iced pumpkin cookies for your snack."

I had her. She wanted to hear no more about any science project, and I knew she was dying to talk.

Inside, Grancie set a plate of iced pumpkin cookies on the breakfast table and started toward the refrigerator for the milk.

"Could I have a cup of tea instead of milk, please? Wouldn't it be nice to have a cup of tea together?"

"I'm sorry, sweetie. Your mom said you didn't sleep well last night, and she said I was not to give you anything with caffeine in it this afternoon, especially if your snack had sugar in it."

"Yes, ma'am. Maybe we can have tea and cookies another day." I put my book bag on the empty chair and sat down. "But it's okay if you'd like tea with your cookies."

"I think I just might have a cup of Darjeeling." She put the teakettle under the faucet. Perfect. In ten minutes she'd be a talking machine. Caffeine loosened Grancie's tongue. "Hope you like the cookies. I had to hide these from your grandfather. He says they're his new favorite."

I asked how she made them, and she told me every detail. I pretended to listen, but I was about as interested in how long to mix the cookies as Grancie was in chromatography.

"Could we work on the afghan today? We could crochet and have a conversation."

"Well, yes, we could do just that. We have about thirty more granny squares to crochet before we can put it all together. Your mom will be so surprised come Christmas."

We finished the cookies, and it wasn't long before we were sitting in our favorite spot in her sunroom. Grancie had grown up in Mississippi, and she liked white wicker and any kind of plant with a flower on it. The ceiling was painted blue like the sky, and the walls were white. It looked like a greenhouse with all her violets and orchids and begonias sitting on every flat surface in that room. It was Grancie's happy place, and I liked it too.

"Your basket is over behind the magazine rack, Julia." She adjusted her chair cushion, got comfortable, and propped her feet up.

Here was my chance—just what I'd been waiting for. "Did you know Dad took me with him to see Mr. Lafferty Monday afternoon?" I picked up my basket and sat down on the sofa, rustling through everything trying to find the granny square I'd worked on last time. I was making my mom an afghan for Christmas.

"He did, did he? Well, what did you think about Mr. Lafferty and that beautiful house?" Grancie paused to count chain stitches.

"I haven't been able to stop thinking about it. I've only seen pictures of houses that big, but I've never seen pictures of anything like Emerald Crest. Do you know about the house? Didn't you go there with G-Pa for parties?" I wound the yarn around my finger and started to crochet.

"Yes, I did." Then Grancie cleared her throat and started her story. When she started, it was like she was reading from some English novel written in the 1800s. "Well, let me tell you about it. Emerald Crest sits atop the highest point on the east side of Sycamore Hill. That old mansion rises in prominence against the horizon as though it grew up there amid the tall pines and cedar trees cradling it, just standing there like a self-proclaimed fortress guarding the town below for the last seventy-five years." She lifted her arm and moved it high above her like she was an actress on a stage delivering her lines.

"Seventy-five years? The house is that old?"

Grancie picked up her yarn and needle and sat back in her wicker rocking chair. "Oh, yes. My mother, your great-grandmother, told me all about the building of that stone manor. Now, Henry Lafferty the First was an Irish immigrant, and it didn't take him long to become a railroad tycoon. And I do believe he made some of his money in the coal industry too. Anyway, before he left Ireland for the United States, he met Colleen. And the moment he looked into her green eyes, his life was changed forever. Moments can do that, you know. He fell in love, married her, and brought her to America. My mother told me after he made his money, Mr. Lafferty decided to build a house that would be a monument for the woman he loved more than life. It had to be a house like no other house ever built."

"You mean like the Taj Mahal?"

"Perhaps it was."

"That's one of the Seven Wonders of the World, you know. A man built it because he loved a woman. I think she was his favorite wife. Probably his other wives didn't like her one bit. But it was no house. It was a tomb and a whole lot

43

of white marble. But it had gardens like Emerald Crest. I've seen pictures." *Hush my mouth. If I start talking, I won't find out anything.* "Mr. Lafferty must have liked green."

"Oh, he did, from the moment he looked into Colleen's green eyes. Not much here would do to build that house, so he went back to Ireland. He found a rare green marble and shipped as much as he could find back to the States. That marble is what you see on the floor of the manor. But then he heard about some green granite up north of here, and he went there and handpicked green granite to match the color of his Irish bride's eyes and had it shipped from the Saco Valley in New Hampshire. He built the exterior walls out of that green stone and then covered the inside walls with the darkest mahogany he could find."

"It was dark, like a forest. But there was a garden room, kind of like this one. I think Mrs. Lafferty must have liked flowers like you do, Grancie. Did she?"

"Oh, yes. Mrs. Lafferty had an eye for anything beautiful. I first met her when Julian T. Russell, Esq., your grandfather, became Mr. Lafferty's attorney. Colleen was a bit older than I was, but she was a green-eyed beauty until the day she died. She was always kind and gracious, and did she ever know how to throw a party. Especially a Christmas party! Why, they were the most lavish Christmas festivities around, and we felt fortunate to be invited. There seemed to be no end to the twinkling lights inside and outside. There were themed Christmas trees in every room—one with angels, one with ornaments from Ireland, another with handblown glass balls, one dressed in silver and another in gold—all different but beautiful. But under each tree were boxes wrapped in red foil and tied with the same red, gold, and green plaid ribbon. I remember that ribbon to this day and wondered where she found it."

"Maybe it came from Ireland too. They like plaid a lot."

"Yes, they do. And Colleen served a feast, not just a delicious meal. And then came the never-ending cups of mulled cider, joyous singing, and fiddle playing. And she would play the piano and sing, and we would join her for some of the carols. And then little Mackenzie would play and sing. She looked like a princess, always in white velvet."

"Who was Mackenzie?"

"She was the Laffertys' only child, and she was a beauty just like her mom—auburn hair and green eyes." Grancie paused again to count the stitches.

"But what about Mr. Lafferty the Second? I thought he was their child."

Grancie shifted in her seat and looked over her glasses at me. "As I was saying, the Christmas parties were truly like something you'd see in the movies. The parties just got bigger and more lavish every year—that is, until the year they stopped."

"You mean she just quit having parties?"

"Yes. I'm not certain that was Colleen's choice, but nevertheless, they stopped. Now, I think you're old enough to hear the rest of this story, but you're not to repeat it. Do you understand?"

"Oh, yes, ma'am. Just like Dad told me not to say anything to anyone about Mr. Lafferty's business."

"True. This is more like attorney-client privilege. And besides, it's their story, not our story to tell."

"I'll never, ever tell. What about Mackenzie?"

Grancie sat back in her chair again, like she was reliving the story. "Well, it seems that one Christmas—oh, I think Mackenzie was about twenty-one. Anyway, she came home for Christmas from her fancy European school, and she brought home more than Christmas presents. Her big surprise was a French husband and a tiny bundle of a baby boy named Henry."

"You mean that baby was Mr. Henry Lafferty the Second?"

"That's what I mean. He is Colleen's grandson. And Mackenzie's arrival with him brought an end to the Christmas parties at Emerald Crest. That was a different time back in those days, Julia. Mr. Lafferty was embarrassed, and he was so disappointed in his daughter. He'd had such high hopes and

45

dreams for his only child." Then Grancie looked straight at me. "All parents are that way, sweetie. And don't you forget it. Don't you break your parents' hearts like Mackenzie did."

"I won't ever. I promise. So what happened?"

"Well, Mr. Lafferty and the Frenchman never got along. I'm not certain any man would have ever lived up to his expectations for a son-in-law. Mr. Lafferty was a hardworking, self-made man, and he looked at this Frenchman as a freeloader. And then it didn't help that little Henry was a sickly baby. The Frenchman didn't hang around long, though, especially when he learned little Henry was deaf—and then Mr. Lafferty offered him a certain sum of money and a one-way ticket on an ocean liner bound for London."

"You mean Mr. Lafferty paid him to leave?"

"Something like that. And you remember your grandfather was a young attorney just starting out in those days, and Mr. Lafferty hired him to get the marriage annulled. That means it was like the marriage never happened. Mr. Lafferty never considered that union honorable in the eyes of the church or the law anyway. Then your grandfather arranged for Mackenzie and the child to take her maiden name, and that's when little Henry became Henry Lafferty the Second."

"So that's why he's not a Junior? Dad didn't tell me that."

"Dads are like that, always trying to protect their daughters from realities that aren't very pleasant. After your grandfather handled all those private details regarding Mackenzie and the baby, Mr. Lafferty trusted him and made him his attorney for life. And even after Mr. Lafferty the First died, your grandfather still took care of everything for young Henry until his retirement and your dad took over."

"So what happened to Mackenzie?"

"Well, that's another long and sad story. It broke Mackenzie's heart when her Frenchman left, but then she had a young child to mother, and she poured every ounce of her love into that little boy. You see, there wasn't much available to help a deaf child in the hills of West Virginia when Henry was small, but there was no lack of love and no shortage of funds to transport him from city to city to see the best doctors. Nothing could be done to restore his hearing, though. Colleen told me once that she and Mackenzie grieved that little Henry would never hear music or the birds in the pines or laughter, but mostly I imagine Mackenzie grieved that he'd never hear the sound of her voice."

"I think she must have played the piano, and I think he must have remembered that when I played for him." I put down my crochet needle. "So where is Mackenzie now, and why does Mr. Lafferty live alone?"

"Well, sweetie, you're just pulling all the sad stories out of me this afternoon. Are you sure you want to hear the rest of this?"

"Oh, yes, ma'am. It's better than the book I'm reading about Beethoven."

"You remember Mackenzie had traveled the world, and then she found herself back in Sycamore Hill with a father who had been shamed and not many friends she could count on. After four years of living with her parents, Mackenzie decided it was time for her and Henry to leave the halls of the green manor. They moved to Richmond, and Henry went to a special school for children who were deaf. They learned sign language together. Colleen told me that Mackenzie feared her son might never hear the sound of her voice, but nothing would stop her from learning how to communicate with him in a way that he would know how much he was loved."

"His mom went to school with him?"

"Colleen said they were never apart. School, church, the park, the playground—wherever young Henry was, Mackenzie was always nearby. Colleen told me that Henry thrived in the Richmond school with other children who were deaf. She talked about their visits home and how his hands and Mackenzie's were always in motion, talking to each other. They returned every Christmas to the green granite house. Now, remember, there were no more lavish parties for all the townsfolk or any of the festive Christmas music, but Henry's grandmother showered that place in colored lights and filled the mansion with the things that delighted him most, like the smell of cinnamon cookies and pine boughs and the sparkling lights that covered the trees in the gardens. To this day, Emerald Crest sparkles at Christmas, at least on the outside. I guess Henry's trying to hang on to what he remembers about Christmas."

"But where is his mom now? Why doesn't she come home for Christmas? She didn't leave Henry and go looking for that good-for-nothing Frenchman, did she? Boy, that would make a good story."

"Julia, for goodness' sake. Where did that question come from? Of course she didn't. She's in heaven, along with both of her parents. So Henry is alone in the world, except for your father and grandfather and Mrs. Schumacher. Your grandfather still visits him on occasion. If I recall, Henry was about your age when she was killed."

"Killed? She was killed?" I hoped I could remember everything Grancie was telling me.

"Yes. It was a truly sad and tragic thing that happened. Mackenzie and Henry were walking to the park in downtown Richmond, and they were talking with their hands, and that requires looking, you know. Henry must have been so excited and not paying attention to the traffic. He stepped into the path of an oncoming car at a busy intersection. Apparently, his mother tried to save him, but the car hit both of them. Mackenzie died right next to Henry, lying in the middle of that busy street. One of Henry's arms was broken, and his hips and legs were badly injured and required surgery. His grandparents rushed to Richmond, and Colleen stayed for weeks until Henry recovered. Your grandfather took care of all the funeral arrangements back here. It was a quiet funeral and private, just for the family and their pastor. That left little Henry to return to Emerald Crest without his mom. His grandmother Colleen brought him home and mothered him for nearly thirty years. She learned sign language so they could communicate, but his grandfather never did. When Colleen died, Henry Lafferty the First and the Second were left to live in silence amid the walls of that green mansion on the hill."

"But Henry the Second didn't have to stay. I would have left. I couldn't live without talking to someone, even if it was with my hands. Why didn't he go back to school in Richmond to be with his friends?"

"Remember, sweetie, this was a different day, and he was severely crippled and unable to hear. He couldn't go alone, and who could go with him? Colleen was torn. She wanted to give Henry the best, but she couldn't leave her husband. Henry rarely left the house even as a child, and by the time he was an adult, he had adjusted to a reclusive life. Your grandfather told me that he immersed himself in a soundless world of books, sculpture, and bird watching, and that he was quite contented with his life. Just because he lives alone doesn't mean that he doesn't know what's going on in the world, you know."

I was about to ask Grancie how long it had been since she had seen Mr. Lafferty, but the doorbell rang.

"That must be your mom. Quick, throw your crocheting in the basket and put it in the corner. We don't want to spoil her surprise. Grab a book like you're reading, and remember, not one word of what I told you to anyone. Your dad knows this, so you can talk to him if you must talk to someone."

"I promise, Grancie. I won't tell a soul. But Mr. Lafferty invited me, and I'm going back to play the piano for him. I'm glad I know this now."

I heard Mom's voice. "Anybody here?"

Grancie answered the door. "We're here, Jennifer. We were out in the sunroom. A beautiful day to be out there."

"Yes. The wind's getting crisp, but you probably have the late-afternoon sunshine coming through all those windows."

"We do, indeed. And the afternoon sunshine is its most

beautiful in late October, don't you think?" Grancie guided Mom to the sunroom.

"Oh, yes. Wish I had time to sit and enjoy it with you for a few minutes. I can't believe I'll be turning the calendar to November soon, and then it'll be Christmas. Gather up your things, Julia. We must hurry. Your dad's getting Jackson from practice, and you and I are picking up pizza and making a salad." She turned to Grancie. "I had an auxiliary meeting this morning before I volunteered at the hospital. We were wondering if you might help us with the table decorations for the Christmas gala. You have that gift with flowers and for making things beautiful. What do you say?"

We walked toward the kitchen and the back door, and I thought of how Grancie and Mr. Lafferty's grandmother could have been good friends. They both liked beautiful things.

"Of course I'll help. We can chat about that later."

Mom opened the door.

"Wait. Did you see Mr. Tucker or any of his family at the hospital today?"

Mom put her arm around me and guided me out the door to the porch. "Only briefly. When I arrived at the hospital this morning, they were preparing to airlift him to Charleston. Funds were even provided for the family's travel so they could be with him. They have specialists there and more advanced equipment. I'm hoping this story will have a happy ending, but he's had a very close call. My heart just goes out to that family. They've already lost so much."

Grancie got that peaceful look on her face. "Yes, but it only takes a moment, just one moment, to change lots of things. That one moment when someone decided to be generous to this family could be a turning point in their lives."

"Hopefully, the moment he gets to Charleston will be the moment that turns things around for them." Mom looked down at me. "Let's go, Jules."

I didn't ask any questions, but I just knew this was the

family that had needed Mr. Lafferty's help. That's why Dad had gone out there to see him, and I was there the moment Mr. Lafferty said yes. He'd come through, but nobody knew except Dad and me and Mrs. Walker. There wouldn't even be one person to say thank you to Mr. Lafferty. But he still did good things anyway.

Mom had often said being grateful showed good manners and upbringing, and that it was the key to being happy. I thought she would expect me to write a thank-you note if someone passed me a tissue during church. Mr. Lafferty was private, probably for good reason, but he surely was robbing somebody of saying thank you.

Mom hugged Grancie. "Thanks, Nancie. You were a lifesaver this afternoon. I know Julia had a good time. She missed you Tuesday night."

Grancie kissed my forehead and winked at me. "Oh, yes. She told me all about chromosomes."

"No, Grancie. Not chromosomes. Chromatography, and don't forget about the chlorophyll and all the green things we talked about. There's always more to a leaf than we can see." I winked back at Grancie.

Chapter Four

FOR THE NEXT FEW DAYS, my head was like Jackson's basketball when he put too much air in it, on its way to exploding. I had way too much information and no way to let it out. The night I came home from Grancie's, I mentioned to Dad that she'd told me about Mr. Lafferty and what happened to Mackenzie, his mother. He frowned and got quiet. I told him I promised Grancie I wouldn't say a word to anyone because it wasn't my story to tell. He didn't exactly smile, but at least the scowl on his face went away. I decided not to mention it again.

But I did ask him that night if he'd called Mrs. Walker about teaching me sign language. Dad said, "I haven't made a decision about that yet. I'll let you know what I've decided the first of November."

"The first of November? But it's the twenty-first of October. What does November first have to do with anything?"

"It has to do with when I'll give you my answer." He was all about postponing. That's what lawyers did. His strategy worked with Jackson, because Jackson was always on to something new or else he just forgot.

I stand at the garden window at Emerald Crest, looking at the pine needles mingling with snowflakes as they drift onto a snow-covered garden. I mentally count the seasons I've watched change through this window—all sixteen years of four seasons, and every one of them beautiful in a different way. But I remember best the first season, and it was winter.

I sigh. I must not stand here reliving my memories any longer. Postponing my apology to Mrs. Finch will not make it easier and only gives her more time for her anger to fester. I can hear her now, stomping around in the dining room, mumbling to herself as I enter. She doesn't look at me, only continuing to arrange silk holly around the brass candlesticks on the table.

"Why couldn't you just have listened to me, Julia? I don't know why you chose to have this gala in the dead of winter. Not a leaf on a tree. Nothing alive and everyone freezing to death in this snow. This could have been such a lavish spring party, but no, you had to do things your way."

I bite my tongue and my lip, hold my hands behind my back, and take a deep breath. "I'm so sorry you didn't get to plan a spring gala of your choosing. Maybe we can persuade Mr. Lafferty to host a spring party another year, and you'll get to plan that one." *I know about postponing things because of Dad. Sometimes problems go away when dealing with them is delayed, and sometimes they don't. He always says wisdom is knowing the difference.*

"Only if I get to plan that party without your help." She refuses to look at me.

"I see your point, Mrs. Finch." I walk away to the garden room before I owe her another apology for something that slipped between my lips.

Ice crystals around the windowpanes frame the view, where more snow clouds are settling on the mountains. I think of children who will enjoy this winter scene and their first spring here, and then a steamy summer before fall temperatures steal the green from the leaves again. No visible leaves today, only bare limbs. But it makes my heart sing to think that Mr. Lafferty wants to have the gala at Christmas. He understands there is beauty in every season, in every leaf, including the ones beneath the snow, gently giving themselves back to the soil, and the unseen buds on the sycamore tree waiting for spring. So why postpone a gala till spring, when we can celebrate at Christmas?

Dad postponed giving me his answer about my taking sign language lessons from Mrs. Walker. But I wasn't like Jackson. I wasn't about to forget, not when I'd set my mind to something. I marked the days on my calendar until November the first. I did everything I could to make the time pass. I practiced the piano and learned some more Christmas songs to play for Mr. Lafferty. I even went with Piper over to Elkins to her dance class, and I went back on Saturday when she auditioned for her part in the Christmas program at the theater. She was the best dancer, and everybody knew it. She was born to be a ballerina.

I also checked out a book in the school library about sign language. That's when I learned about body language and how we communicate with our faces and expressions. I'd already figured that out. All I needed to do was look at Dad to know when I'd said enough about something. And I remembered Mr. Lafferty's face and his hands and how sometimes his hands moved fast like he was angry or excited and sometimes they were gentle like he was tired or thinking. And his face said so much, even without opening his mouth.

I thought about Mr. Lafferty and about my next visit, but I kept my thoughts to myself. Thank heavens Piper didn't ask me any more questions about the green mansion. She was into sugar plum fairies and dance costumes. I held my breath every day at school, hoping Angus and Gary had forgotten all about our conversation about ghosts and caves. I could breathe when Halloween was over and they didn't ask about the Halloween story I'd told them I was writing.

But now I would finally know if Mrs. Walker would teach me sign language.

When I reminded Dad at breakfast that it was the first day of November, he looked at his watch and then at me. "I believe it will still be the first day of November this evening."

After school, I went straight upstairs to my room. Our house was part old and part new. My parents had bought this place when they got married, and they'd been working on it ever since. They had lots of stories. Dad wanted a house in town so he could walk to work and to the courthouse, but Mom wanted to live in the country. She wanted a big yard so she could plant vegetables and raise chickens, and she really wanted a barn.

They settled on this stacked-stone house on the edge of town and tore down walls and added on rooms. Mom wanted a brand-new kitchen and a big family room. She liked it that she could be in the kitchen and keep her eye on Jackson and me. She didn't get the barn she wanted, but she got a carriage house. She made it into a studio where she could go and paint and not have to clean up. Dad helped her make a garden for the herbs she liked for cooking and some vegetables, and they planted fruit trees. We had pears and apples and peaches and even figs.

They tried raising chickens before I was born. Dad told funny stories about things they'd find in the chicken coop and about the rooster that crowed all night and went missing. Mom always thought the neighbors had stewed that bird. Dad said that's when she gave up on chickens.

Jackson's room, my room, and the guest room were all upstairs. The good part was I didn't have to share a bathroom. My room was on the corner, with windows where I could see the carriage house out back and the peach and apple trees from the side windows. The apples were almost gone. One more gusty day like today, and no more apples until next October.

I loved my room. Everything was blue, just like I liked it—light-blue walls, blue curtains, blue pillows, and the blue quilt that had been my other grandmother's. I didn't really remember her because she'd died when I was just a baby.

The windows shone with light all day, but they didn't leave much wall space for bookshelves. I had about an acre of books. But the best part of my room was my desk. Grancie and G-Pa had given it to me for my tenth birthday. It had belonged to my great-grandfather, and it was about the size of King William County—a maple roll-top with lots of drawers and slots and cubbies. It even had two secret compartments and was about the only thing in my room that wasn't blue.

I stayed in my room reading until Mom called me for dinner, then went straight to the stone fireplace when I got downstairs. Jackson had built a bonfire in it. Building fires was one thing he was good for, which I appreciated after the chill in my room. I warmed my hands and turned around. "Jackson, you build such good fires that you'd be a great pyromaniac."

He smiled. He thought it was a compliment because it was a big word and he didn't even know what a pyromaniac was.

Dad was already home, so we all took our seats at the table. Steaming bowls of homemade chili, hot buttered corn bread, and apple salad. My kind of supper on the first night in November.

Dad didn't even give me a chance to ask. "Julia, let's have a pleasant meal. Your mom has gone out of her way to prepare something we all like. Then we'll have a powwow around the fireplace. It's still November first."

That didn't sound good. I didn't think Dad knew what a real powwow was. It was a time when the Indians partied—dancing, eating, singing, being friendly. But when Dad said powwow, it just meant we were going to have a talk, kind of like a come-to-Jesus meeting. And it didn't much sound like I would like it.

We finished our meal. It was my night to help Mom clear the table, and Dad sent Jackson for another couple of logs to put on the fire. By the time Mom and I finished in the kitchen, they were into the first quarter of a basketball game on television. Dad sat in his lounge chair, and Jackson was draped over the entire sofa, so I sat in the rocking chair near the fire. That way, Dad had to look in my direction while he watched TV.

I sat up straight and stared in his direction, but I didn't say anything.

Finally, at the commercial, Dad turned to me. "Julia, you look like you might be waiting for the dentist to call you back to fill your tooth. Are you in pain?"

"Not exactly. I'm just waiting for the powwow."

"Oh, that's right. The powwow." Dad looked at his watch. "Only four hours and seventeen minutes until November the second."

"We don't really need a powwow. Just tell me. Is Mrs. Walker going to teach me or not?"

"No, she's not going to teach—"

I knew it. I knew I wasn't going to like this. I began my argument before he could finish. "But I have time. It won't take away from my studies or anything else."

"That's not the problem, Julia. She doesn't have time. But ... she suggested ..." He pulled out a small package wrapped in brown paper from under his chair. "This."

"What is that? A peace offering since I don't get the only thing in the world I really want?"

"Not exactly. Why don't you open it?"

I got up and took it from Dad's hand. It was a package addressed to me. I opened it. "Oh, wow!" I yanked off the cellophane. "This is a great peace offering."

Jackson roused from the sofa. "What is it?"

"It's a set of DVDs that will teach me sign language."

Jackson rolled his eyes. "Like I told you. You could teach yourself."

58

"Yes, I can, and I can learn as fast as I want to. I won't have to wait on lessons. I'm already learning to fingerspell from the book I checked out of the school library. This is the best. Did Mrs. Walker give it to me? I should write her a note."

Mom said, "Maybe you could write her a note for suggesting it to your dad. He ordered it for you."

"But why didn't you tell me? Why did I have to wait until November first?"

Dad threw up his hands. "Because I had to wait until it got here. Didn't you like the surprise and enjoy the anticipation?"

"I love the surprise, but I don't like not knowing something. Thank you. Thank you so much. Just think, Dad, if I learn how to sign, you may not need Mrs. Walker anymore." I stood up and signed *Thank you very much* to Mom and Dad.

Dad surprised me. He signed *You're welcome* right back.

"Do you know sign language, Dad?"

"Oh, no. Just a few basic signs, and I can fingerspell a little. But I'm slow. Maybe you can teach me."

"I will. You can count on it. May I go upstairs and try out the DVDs right now?"

"Yes. Go to it, girl. I want to watch the ball game."

I was halfway up the stairs when the phone rang. I hoped it was Piper so I could tell her about my surprise. But I knew it wasn't her when I heard Dad say, "No, it's not too late, Mrs. Walker."

I stood on the step and listened. Why was Mrs. Walker calling? Maybe she'd changed her mind about teaching me.

"Oh no. When? Can you let him know I'm on my way? I'll call someone to get it repaired, and we'll get it boarded up tonight. I won't be able to get anybody to replace it until tomorrow, though." Dad paused. "By the way, the package came today, and Julia's very happy. The DVDs won't play fast enough for her. I can imagine she'll be fast-forwarding." Dad paused again. "Thank you for letting me know. I'll get right out to Mr. Lafferty's."

He hung up. "Jackson, get your shoes on and get your coat. I need you to go with me to Mr. Lafferty's. He has a broken window, and we need to board it up for the night until someone can make the repairs tomorrow. I should change my clothes. I'll get the toolbox and a piece of plyboard from the shed. Oh, and get us a couple of flashlights."

Dad had been called before to go out to Mr. Lafferty's, but it was the first time he'd ever said why and the first time he asked Jackson to go with him.

Jackson grumbled. "So much for the ball game."

Mom replied, "And so much for good deeds, Jackson. I think it's been a while since you've done one."

I practically catapulted myself down the stairs. "I'll go. I need to do a good deed too. I know where the flashlights are. I'll get my jacket."

Mom interrupted. "Julia, it's almost your bedtime, and I don't think you'd be much help with this one."

Dad was walking out of the room. "Your mom's right. We're just going to nail up some plyboard and maybe clean up a little."

"But I could help clean up and hold the flashlight, and I could see Mr. Lafferty."

"Not tonight. Besides, I doubt he wants to see anyone tonight. I'll need to go out again tomorrow afternoon to make certain the repairs are done. You can go then."

Mom added, "Yes, and maybe you could go upstairs and learn a few signs. Mr. Lafferty will be impressed that you're learning to communicate with him." Mom liked to change the subject. It had worked when I was about five, but not anymore.

But there was nothing to be done about it. I went upstairs and pouted and practiced my signs.

Mom was adding pecans to the oatmeal and Dad was pouring himself a cup of coffee when I came down the next morning. They were talking, so I stayed in the hallway to listen.

"This is the second window in the last couple of months. I think it's time to make some changes."

"What kind of changes?"

"I don't need to be relying on Mrs. Walker for phone calls at night. So, the first thing I need to do is to get a TTY at home. I have the one at the office, and Mr. Lafferty can call me there during the day. But he should be able to get me at home any time. I'll get Robbie on that today."

"That's a good idea, but I don't know what else you could do. You know he doesn't want anyone living there."

"Mrs. Schumacher is there during the day, but I think there needs to be a different kind of security system, or maybe someone on the property to watch things at night for a while."

"You're positive this is vandalism?"

"Well, the first time it was a limb through a downstairs window. So, I guess it's possible that wind could have caused that one. But not last night. We're talking about a good-sized rock thrown through his bedroom window. Probably happened about dusk. The rest of the house was dark, and he was working in his room upstairs with the lights on. He wrote a note saying he saw two figures running into the woods right after it happened."

"Apparently they didn't want to hurt him."

I heard Jackson opening the door to his room. I didn't want him to catch me eavesdropping on our parents' conversation, so I dropped my backpack loudly in the hallway, walked into the breakfast room, and acted like I'd only heard the part about hurting Mr. Lafferty.

"Who doesn't want to hurt somebody?"

Dad sat down at the table and looked at Mom like he was asking for permission to tell me. He didn't like oatmeal, so Mom put a plate of scrambled eggs and toast in front of him.

"You might as well tell her," she said. "She won't stop asking questions, you know." Then she set my cup of tea down at my place.

"Thank you, ma'am. You can tell me anything. I'm very confidential. And besides, Jackson knows, doesn't he?"

Dad smeared peach preserves on his toast. "Well, it seems some mean-spirited people are taunting Mr. Lafferty. He's had a couple of windows broken lately."

"But why would anybody do that?"

"Remember, I'm an attorney. I deal with criminals and mean-spirited people almost every day. And believe me, there is no shortage of people who would do something like that just for fun."

"You know what Grancie would say about that. She'd say that was a dump-truck load of pure devilment." I stirred my tea and sprinkled more brown sugar on my oatmeal. "But they won't hurt Mr. Lafferty, will they?"

"I hope not. But he could have been hurt last night. Someone hurled a rock through an upstairs window while he was sitting at his worktable carving. His bedroom light was the only light on in the house."

"He carves birds in his bedroom?"

"Not the big pieces. He does that outside in his workshop. But sometimes when he's working on the fine details of a small piece, he carves at night in his bedroom upstairs."

Jackson came in, sat down, and started shoveling oatmeal into his mouth. "Yeah, you should have seen it. That is one big bedroom, and there was glass everywhere. But we got it cleaned up."

I imagined Mr. Lafferty had been covered in glass before he knew what happened. He couldn't have heard the glass shattering and didn't know to protect himself. "What are you going to do, Dad? You have to do something. He shouldn't be living there alone."

"You're right. But Mr. Lafferty likes his privacy, and he is very independent."

Jackson practically heaved his milk down his throat. He made the gross-meter tick, the way he ate. "Yeah, I've heard plenty of tales about that place and about Mr. Lafferty, how he's like some kind of phantom or troll. And I've heard about money being buried in the caves around there."

Those were the same things Angus and Gary had said. "You never told me about that, Jackson."

"That's because you were a girl and a baby. Girls don't talk about that kind of stuff. Besides, I didn't want you having nightmares and screaming at night." Jackson wiped his mouth.

"How would you know what girls talk about, and besides, it didn't keep you from telling me that scarecrows come to life at night and steal little girls."

Dad put down his coffee. "Enough. This kind of talk is exactly why Mr. Lafferty lives like a recluse. He was made fun of as a child, and don't think he doesn't know about these stories about himself and his property. He's aware. So he chooses to live his life in privacy."

I looked at Dad. "Well, maybe if he didn't live like that and people got to know him … ?"

"That's not likely to happen, Julia. And none of this talk leaves this table, you hear? Both of you. And none of what you saw last night, Jackson. I'm Mr. Lafferty's attorney and his friend, and I'd like it to stay that way. You're both old enough now to be trusted with some information, and I'm counting on you."

Jackson spoke first. "Yes, sir. My lips are sealed."

"Mine too. But I have a question."

Mom looked at Dad. "I'm not surprised."

"Is any of that stuff true? That part about the ghost and the caves and the money?"

"Of course not. People have been telling tales about

Emerald Crest since I was a kid. When there's a bit of mystery, then people start making up stuff, and the next generation adds to the tales. And before long there are more legends than truth. Now, it is true there are some caves on the property, but caves are all around these parts, some probably still undiscovered. But I can assure you no one has buried any money in the caves on Emerald Crest property. That property has been owned by the Laffertys for three generations."

"And no bones of people who got lost trying to find the money?"

"What? Bones? Where'd you get that idea?"

Hush my mouth. Jesus, forgive me. What I'm about to say is the truth, just not the whole truth. "I probably read something like that in a book."

"Then you're reading the wrong books." Mom got up from the table. "Need to get going."

"But I have another question: If Mrs. Walker wasn't there, how did she know what happened?"

"It has to do with the way Mr. Lafferty uses a special telephone, and I don't have time to explain that right now. Later." Dad took his plate and cup to the sink.

"Okay, if you won't answer that one, then I have one more question."

"Spit it out."

"Last night you said you were going back out to Mr. Lafferty's this afternoon and I could go with you. Are we still going?"

Dad smiled at me. "Girl, I tell you, you will be one fine attorney someday with an assumptive close like that one. Yes, I am going back this afternoon and if your mom says it's okay, you may go with me."

"Mom?"

"Yes, you may go. I'll pick you up from school and take you to your dad's office."

"Thank you. I can't wait to sign to Mr. Lafferty. I already know a few signs to show I have good manners, and I already know how to fingerspell, just not so fast."

Dad patted me on the head. "Yes, and I imagine that every word will be spelled correctly."

"Yes, sir. But, I don't think I want to be an attorney. Hanging around scoundrels all the time doesn't interest me."

Dad laughed. "Yeah, I hang around a lot of those, and we hang some of them too."

Mom threw the dishrag at Dad. "Ben. Don't tell her that. Tell her that's not true."

Dad caught the dishrag before it dampened his shirt. "Your mother's right. We don't hang people, no matter what. And remember, I do get to hang around some mighty fine people—people who make a real difference in the world. People like Mr. Lafferty, whose heart pumps pure goodness."

"Yes, and I'll be glad to see him. I have two new Christmas songs I can play for him. I think he really likes Christmas songs. Do I have time now to practice for a few minutes?"

Mom said, "Five minutes. That's it. Then we must go. Get moving, Jackson."

Yes. Finally. I was returning to Emerald Crest. I would play for Mr. Lafferty, and I would sign to him. I was mostly curious about Mr. Lafferty. Curious about things like what it was like to be deaf, and what his secret gift was that I didn't know about yet, and why he was still generous and kind when almost everybody was mean to him. I didn't think my heart pumped goodness like Dad said Mr. Lafferty's did, but I wanted Mr. Lafferty to know not everybody was a scoundrel.

Chapter Five

PIPER WASN'T NEARLY AS EXCITED about learning sign language until I told her my idea: If we both knew sign language, then we could communicate when we weren't supposed to be talking in class, and it would be our own secret language, so no one else would know what we were saying. I started teaching her the alphabet during morning break. I could tell she was going to be really good at signing. She was smart, and she signed like she danced. She asked me how to sign words that I didn't know yet. I invited her for an overnight on the weekend so she could see my DVDs and we could learn some secret signs to start using right away. Mom wouldn't mind. Piper was like another daughter. And besides, having Piper around kept me out of Mom's business.

Right after school, Mom took me to Dad's office. Mrs. Mason, Dad's secretary, greeted us and told us Dad was still in a meeting. "Jennifer, if you need to do something else, I'll be here with Julia. Ben has a four-thirty appointment with Mr. Lafferty, so we have a bit of time. She can have a snack from the break room, and Ben asked me to show her the TTY."

"That would be so helpful, Robbie. I have errands to run, and that'll give me a bit of extra time." Mom looked at me. "Amuse yourself, Julia. Mrs. Mason probably has business to tend to."

"Yes, ma'am."

Mom hugged me and was out the door.

"Mrs. Mason, you said something about a TTY and Dad wanting me to see it. What's that?"

"What about a snack first? Aren't you hungry?" She led me to the break room.

I spied the box on the counter. "Could I have a donut?"

"They're stale."

"That's okay. I like stale donuts. I'll just put it in the microwave." I wrapped the donut in a napkin. "And could I please have a cup of coffee?"

Mrs. Mason looked like I might have asked her for an octopus or something. "It was made a few hours ago, and are you sure you're even allowed to drink coffee?"

"I drink hot tea mostly, with lots of milk, but on special occasions I'm allowed coffee. And today is a special occasion. I'm going to see Mr. Lafferty. And coffee would be really good with a donut."

Mrs. Mason reached for a mug. "And I'm guessing this mug should be mostly milk too, like you have your tea."

"Oh, no, ma'am. I have milk with my tea, but I have cream with my coffee."

She opened the fridge and reached for a carton of half and half and started to pour.

"More, please."

Her eyebrows were raised when she turned to look at me and kept pouring. "Enough yet?"

"Yes, ma'am. That will be perfect with three sugars."

She handed me three packets of sugar and a spoon. "Perhaps you should stay here until you finish your coffee. Then you can join me at my desk."

It took no time to finish my snack, and I was back in the lobby with Mrs. Mason. "Thank you so much, Mrs. Mason. I really enjoyed my snack."

"You're welcome, Julia. And the coffee?"

"Perfect."

"Why don't you come right over here to my desk, and I'll show you the TTY. Your dad told me you wanted to know about communicating with Mr. Lafferty, and this is how we do it." She pulled up the side chair next to her. "Sit here so you can see." She pointed to a telephone on her desk.

"It just looks like a telephone with a keyboard to me."

"That's pretty much what it is. It's called a TTY, a text telephone. Do you see the screen?"

"Yes, ma'am."

"Mr. Lafferty has a phone just like this one at his house. And when he needs to talk with your dad, he dials our office number, types what he'd like to say, and it appears right here on this screen."

"And then you answer and type back?"

"That's about it."

"So, Mr. Lafferty can only communicate with someone who knows sign language or someone who has one of these?"

"There is another way for him to use the telephone. Let's say we didn't have this TTY and he needed to talk to your dad. He could use his TTY to call a special number for a relay service. Then the relay service would call your dad and voice Mr. Lafferty's message. The relay operator would type your dad's response for Mr. Lafferty to see on his TTY. But Mr. Lafferty doesn't like to use the relay service."

"I know. He doesn't like other people in his business."

About that time, Dad came out of his office with two men, and they left. Their faces said they might have had one of Dad's powwows and it didn't turn out like the one we had last night.

"Hey, Jules! I see you're learning all about the TTY."

"Yes, sir."

Mrs. Mason said, "And soon you'll have one of these at your house. I ordered it today."

Dad grabbed his coat. "Great. We should be on our way. Don't want to keep Mr. Lafferty waiting."

I moved the chair back to where it was. "Thank you for your time this afternoon, Mrs. Mason. And thank you for teaching me about the TTY."

"You're welcome. You can come by and have coffee and donuts with me anytime. No one else around here eats stale donuts." She grinned at Dad.

Dad pinched my ear, and we were out the door. "Coffee? You had coffee and a donut? I may lock you in the car when we get to Emerald Crest."

"No need. I didn't eat but two bites of the donut and the coffee was mostly cream. I'm tame."

"We'll pick up Mrs. Walker and be on our way. I need her today because I must have a conversation with Mr. Lafferty about making some changes regarding security."

"I'm still reading my sign language book, so I won't be a bother. And I'll be happy to play the piano for him if he remembers." I pulled the book from my bag.

"Oh, he remembers. I told him earlier this morning you were coming with me."

We picked up Mrs. Walker just like before, and she had no more than closed the door when I started thanking her for suggesting the DVDs and showed her my sign language book and told her I knew what a TTY was.

Dad said, "I think the coffee's kicking in. Just look at your book, please. I need to speak with Mrs. Walker. I may need her to be more than an interpreter this afternoon."

We were pulling up the hill on the long driveway when they finished talking. Mrs. Walker turned to me in the back seat. "It's important that you know I am an interpreter. That means I should behave more like the TTY, just as a conduit of information and communication between your father and Mr.

Lafferty. I do not express my opinions, and I don't insert myself into their conversation. Do you remember how that went from last time we were here?"

"Yes, ma'am."

"But today, your father has asked me not only to interpret but also to express my own opinions since he knows that Mr. Lafferty is my friend and I'm very concerned about him right now."

"I don't want anything bad to happen to Mr. Lafferty. He's had enough bad things in his life."

Dad parked the car, and we climbed the front steps. He let me ring the bell. Lights flickered in several places inside the house.

This time, Mrs. Schumacher answered the door. I'd heard Mom say she was the housekeeper who came to clean and do the cooking. She introduced herself to me and then pointed down the hall to the glassed-in room where the piano was and said, "Come with me, and I'll get Mr. Lafferty. He's in the garden."

"Wait," Dad said. "If he's in the garden, could we watch him from the window for just a moment?"

"Certainly, Mr. Russell, but he might have seen the lights flicker when you rang the bell."

"Try to stay quiet, Julia, and don't make any sudden movements." We practically tiptoed down the hollow hall into the garden room. There stood the piano, and beyond was the garden.

The afternoon sun was so bright that Mr. Lafferty hadn't noticed the flashing lights when the bell rang, and so bright I could barely make out more than his silhouette. He sat in his wheelchair on the brick garden path with his back to the window.

Dad motioned for me to step closer.

I did, and I could see color. Mr. Lafferty and his plaids. He had a plaid blanket across his shoulders and a different plaid tam on his head. But I noticed his right arm was stretched straight out from his body and his palm was up.

Then I saw it—his amazing gift. I stepped even closer to the window just to be certain what I thought I saw was real. It was. A tiny chickadee fed from his hand, and another one perched on his left shoulder. And then more came. Birds fluttered all around him like bees to a honeycomb.

I turned around to Dad. "The birds? That's his special gift? The birds coming to him like that?"

"Yes. Never knew anybody who could feed wild birds out of his hand. That's why he can sculpt them. He studies them up close and feels their lightness and their softness."

"How did he learn to do that? Is he like a bird whisperer or something? I want to learn to do that too!"

I could have watched Mr. Lafferty feed those birds until next Tuesday, but Dad nodded, and Mrs. Schumacher opened the door to the garden. The second the birds flew, Mr. Lafferty swiveled around. He saw us, brushed the birdseed from his hand, waved, and started pushing his chair to the doorway. As Mr. Lafferty rolled into the room, Mrs. Schumacher signed and asked Dad, "Would you like to meet in the dining room as usual?"

Dad hesitated. "You know, I think we'll just sit right here this afternoon." Mrs. Walker interpreted Dad's answer. I had at least a gazillion questions about learning to feed birds from my hand, but I knew better than to ask.

Mr. Lafferty signed something back really fast, and Mrs. Schumacher nodded in agreement. "Mr. Lafferty would enjoy having you join him for a cup of tea, and wouldn't you know, I just baked some scones this afternoon, and I have freshly made strawberry jam." Then she turned to me. "Julia? That was your name, wasn't it?"

"Yes, ma'am."

"Would you like a glass of milk?"

"Oh, no, thank you. I'd really like a cup of tea." I glanced at my dad. I knew he was adding up a cup of coffee, a cup of tea, a stale donut, and a fresh scone with jam in one afternoon.

"Thank you, Mrs. Schumacher, but maybe you could put

mostly milk in Julia's teacup since she's already had coffee this afternoon. Too much caffeine for seventy pounds of girlishness. I must say, though, my daughter does enjoy her tea."

Mrs. Walker signed everything Dad said. I looked at Mr. Lafferty the whole time, and he grinned just a little about the tea.

"Oh, she'll enjoy this. It's Irish afternoon tea, and it's perfect for a November day."

Mrs. Schumacher disappeared into the kitchen. Dad and Mrs. Walker sat on the sofa, and he motioned for me to sit in the chair near the piano. I hadn't really looked at the room so much the first time I was here because I was more interested in the piano and the ivory keys. But when I looked around, I saw every piece of furniture in that room was covered in flowers—big fluffy chairs, two sofas, a stool, and too many pillows to count. Green marble, like Grancie had said, covered the floor.

Mr. Lafferty wheeled his chair right in front of Dad, and he couldn't see me. I fidgeted because I knew if I waited they'd start talking, and I'd never have my chance. So I got up out of the flowered chair I had sunk into and walked over to where Mr. Lafferty could see me. He looked at me like he was afraid I might hug him again. But I didn't. I stood there and signed *How are you?*

Mr. Lafferty looked like I might have thrown a plate of spaghetti at him. He jerked his head back, and if eyes could talk, I would have had an earful. Then he signed *Fine, how are you?*

I answered. Then he started signing fast, and I didn't understand a thing. Mrs. Walker stepped in to interpret. He was curious about how I knew those signs and how much sign language I knew.

I explained I had DVDs that were teaching me the basics. Then I signed *What is your sign name, please?*

He smiled and made the sign for the letter *H.* His eyes and the movement of his head asked me if I knew the sign.

I signed *Yes* and started showing him I knew how to fingerspell the entire alphabet.

He fingerspelled the alphabet with me and signed *Good,*

good when we finished. Then he made the sign for *H* again, pressed his two fingers to his lips, and then moved them to the left side of his chest, right over his heart. *My sign name.* He repeated and then pointed to me.

I signed his name and then *I like that.*

That's when Dad interrupted our conversation, and Mrs. Walker became the interpreter. I plopped down into the chair by the piano again and watched and listened. When they began talking about the broken window, immediately Mr. Lafferty started pushing himself toward the front hallway and motioned for them to follow.

Dad turned to me. "He wants me to see the repaired window. You stay here." He and Mrs. Walker followed Mr. Lafferty to the hallway, where two wooden panels on the wall opened up and showed an elevator. I'd never thought about how Mr. Lafferty got upstairs. I'd guessed he just lived downstairs.

They disappeared into that elevator, and I had time to look around the room. Grancie had said Colleen Lafferty liked flowers and beautiful things, and she was right. Flowers were everywhere—fabric, paintings on the wall opposite the windows, fresh flowers on the table in the corner, and birds. Small carved birds looked like they'd just alighted on the tables and on the shelves at the other end of the room.

Since they were all small, I imagined the wooden birds were the first Mr. Lafferty had carved as a child. I just knew if I pulled one of those bird books off the shelf there would be wood shavings in its pages. He had touched birds, had felt the softness of their feathers, but he'd never heard a cardinal song or the chirp of a chickadee. I wondered when and how he'd learned to feed them.

Then there were other books on the shelves, stacked on the floor, and on the tables—novels, books on gardening, lots of travel books, and books about Ireland and Scotland, books to take him to places he could never go. I fancied that his grandmother had told him all about growing up in Ireland. This room was Mr. Lafferty's window to the world. I decided his grandmother had thought if he couldn't hear, then she would make everything he saw beautiful.

Then I spied framed photographs on the bookshelves in the corner. I got up out of my chair and walked closer. I couldn't tell if they were pictures of his grandmother or of his mother, Mackenzie. They looked like the same woman—same hair, same eyes, but not quite the same. And then there was the picture of a little boy in a suit next to this woman. That had to be Mr. Lafferty. I was just about to pick it up to look closer when I heard the elevator. I moved quickly back to my chair.

They entered the room and took their seats. Almost at the same time, Mrs. Schumacher came in through the door to the kitchen, served our tea and scones, and disappeared again.

Dad made small talk until we finished our tea, then started in on his mission. He told Mr. Lafferty that he was very worried about the broken-window incidents and that he was having a TTY installed at our home. Dad said, "I thought all this was just a bit of mischief, but my concern is growing since this is the second episode this month, and this one came through your bedroom window while your light was on."

Mr. Lafferty said he wasn't too bothered by the first one, but the second one with a rock flying through his window had kept him from sleeping last night.

Dad suggested everything from wooden shutters to an updated security system with more nightlights and cameras to someone living at the house full time. Mrs. Walker interpreted and announced when she was inserting her own opinions. Everything she said backed up Dad's ideas. She explained that during this approaching holiday season of the year, there was always more reported crime, and she didn't want Mr. Lafferty to get hurt.

Mr. Lafferty refused the idea of shutters, and why wouldn't he? What world would he have left without windows? He had no interest in someone living there, and he argued that another person in the house would be very little protection from rocks thrown through windows anyway. He agreed to think about a new security system and asked Dad to check into it. But when Dad mentioned having someone patrol the property at night for a few weeks, Mr. Lafferty said yes.

I think he agreed because Dad told him Mr. Hornsby could really use the work since he had been laid off from the mill in Elkins. Dad reminded him Mr. Hornsby just lived down the road, had four children to feed, and Christmas was coming. Like Dad said, "Mr. Lafferty's heart pumps goodness." They agreed that Dad would call Mr. Hornsby and get him started right away and that he could use Mr. Lafferty's studio as a place to come in from the cold when he wasn't patrolling the grounds.

Mr. Lafferty reminded Dad that the terrain was rugged and that Mr. Hornsby would need a vehicle. Dad agreed to check on renting an all-terrain vehicle. Before they finished, Dad summarized his assignments, and I could tell he was satisfied and wanted to leave before Mr. Lafferty changed his mind. I had been quiet because I was learning stuff, but I wasn't about to leave without playing the piano.

Mr. Lafferty was the most interesting person I had ever met. The only people I knew were a lot like me. They might have been taller or shorter, or brunette, or smarter, or dumber, or interested in other things, but we were so much alike. And none of us were like him, with his own language and feeding birds out of his hand and carving birds. Mr. Lafferty was just a whole heap of mystery, and I wanted to know more and more about him.

I stepped up to Mr. Lafferty again and signed *I* and pointed to the piano. It wasn't really sign language, but he understood and smiled. I signed *Learned two new songs*. Mr. Lafferty almost did a wheelie and went straight to the curve of the piano. When he got in position, he waved for me to play.

I sat down and began to play "Deck the Halls," and I followed that with "O Christmas Tree." When I finished, he signed *Again, please.* I repeated both songs. Then he asked me to play and sing "Silent Night." His hand was on the piano just like before, and he looked at my face. As I started to sing, his mouth formed the same words. He understood. I just knew he remembered his mother and his grandmother singing and playing for him. All the tension from talking about shattered windows and the need for security disappeared from his face. He was peaceful. He asked me to sing it one more time.

Dad said, "Time to go, Julia. I'm sure Mr. Lafferty must be tired. He didn't get much sleep last night."

I got up from the piano. My good manners had been on parade long enough. If I didn't ask, then I would for certain never know, and there was so much I wanted to know about his world. So I walked right up to him and said, "Mr. Lafferty, I'd like to come to your house more often. And I'd really like you to teach me sign language. Mrs. Walker doesn't have time to teach me, and I really want to learn more than anything. Watching the DVDs helps, but I think you could teach me a whole lot better." Mrs. Walker signed what I said with all the excitement she could muster.

I waited for Dad to interrupt, but he didn't. Mr. Lafferty lowered his head and closed his eyes. I wondered if he was praying about it. No use in saying anything else, because he wasn't looking. I stopped up my ears when I'd heard enough; he just closed his eyes.

Finally, he raised his head. His eyes and his lips were smiling when he signed *Yes, I will teach you sign language.*

I immediately signed *Thank you very much.* I wasn't like Dad, and I wasn't about to quit while I was ahead. "And would you teach me how to carve birds?" Mrs. Walker interpreted that.

That was the first time I heard him laugh, even if it was just a weird chuckle. He nodded his head. *If I teach you to carve birds, you will have to agree to play the piano and learn my favorites.*

I knew he remembered. He even had favorites. "Yes, sir, I will. I will learn your favorites and play them for you. Thank you so much. I promise to be a good student." I stepped nearer and gave him another hug. Hugging was the one thing I needed to teach Mr. Lafferty, but I thought he could learn.

He followed us to the front door, and Dad said his good-byes. I turned and waved and formed an *H* with my right hand, pressed it to my lips, and then to my heart.

Mr. Lafferty cocked his head just like one of those chick-adees he was feeding. He looked so curious, like he didn't know what to sign, so he just smiled and waved goodbye.

That was the day Mr. Henry Lafferty the Second became H to me.

Chapter Six

SEVERAL DAYS LATER, PIPER AND I were in my room practicing sign language. Mom had moved an old bench from her studio so that we both could sit in front of the computer at my desk. We watched the video and repeated the signs. After a while, I stopped the video, and we used our hands like the flashcards we used to learn our multiplication tables. I would sign something, she would voice it, and then we'd switch.

Piper made sign language look like ballet. Her fingers were shorter than mine and twice as graceful, but I was catching on quicker. Signing just came naturally to me.

Piper got up, pirouetted across the wooden floor, and plopped down on the bed. "I need a break."

"Yeah, me too. I just want to learn a few more signs before tomorrow, but I'll do that later."

"Emerald Crest sounds like a castle. I hope I get to see it."

"It is like a castle, and I want you to go with me. Dad already said I could go tomorrow, and he's working out a schedule for my weekly visits. I hope you can go with me soon. But for now, I can't ask anything about anything. I'm still sitting on the edge of trouble for not talking to my dad before I asked Mr. Lafferty to teach me to sign and to carve birds."

"But you're going back tomorrow?"

"Yes." *Jesus, forgive me for breaking my word, but Piper won't tell.* "Mr. Lafferty's window was broken the other night. Dad's going out to check on it, and he's taking Mr. Hornsby. He's the new man who will work for Mr. Lafferty at night when he's there alone. He's supposed to walk around the property and keep everything safe."

"Safe? Is Mr. Lafferty in danger?"

"Oh, no. He's not in danger." I knew I had said too much, and worse than that, I had said the wrong thing.

"Did someone break the window on purpose?"

Now, Jesus, please forgive me again. I've thought better of it, and I shouldn't be breaking promises. Now I must fib to cover up the first one. "Probably it was just the wind. His house sits on a high hill, you know."

"Yeah. That can happen." She turned around and looked at me. "You're always wanting to learn new stuff, Julia. Tell me again why you want to learn to sign to that old man who lives out there." Then Piper walked over to my dresser and picked up my hairbrush.

I watched that brush go through her hair like it was silk threads. "I don't know exactly. Why do you want to learn to dance?"

"I don't know exactly, either. I just know I couldn't imagine not dancing."

"I think it's the same with me. After I met Mr. Lafferty, I knew I wanted to learn sign language so I could talk to him. He's different in an interesting way."

"But carving birds? Why do you want to carve birds?"

"Because that's what Mr. Lafferty likes. I figured if I carved birds with him that he would want to spend time with me."

"But you already said he likes you to play the piano. You could just play the piano to spend time with him." She put the brush down and turned around.

"It's not the same. I think I should learn to like what he likes. And I think carving will be interesting. You should see his birds. He must really like cardinals. They're everywhere in that house, and it's always a pair carved out of one piece of wood. Just think about it: you start with a block of wood and whittle away until a bird appears." I looked at my hair in the mirror, picked up the brush, and put it down. I could dump a bottle of conditioner on my head and brush my hair until next April, and it wouldn't look like Piper's. My spongy curls would never be silky.

"Carving birds can't be that easy. You could cut your finger off, and then you wouldn't be able to sign anymore."

"Yeah, but I'll be careful. I've seen some scars on Mr. Lafferty's hands, probably made with carving tools."

The doorbell rang. I went to the window. A delivery truck was parked in the driveway. "Come on, let's go downstairs."

"Is it my mother or do you have company?"

"No, just a delivery. But I think I know what it is. Let's go see." I bounced down the stairs, but Piper floated down step by step like a Hollywood movie queen making her grand entrance.

Mom was just closing the front door. She set the box on the table in the hallway. "Hey, girls. Done with your studying?"

"Yes, ma'am."

"That's good. Piper, your mom just called. She's on her way and in a hurry. You should probably gather your things."

"Yes, ma'am. I have everything right here in my backpack." She set it on the floor in the hallway.

I read the lettering on the box. "I knew it. It's the TTY. Let's open it?"

"It would be better to wait until your dad gets home. We don't need any parts to go missing."

"But, we could just open it. I want to show Piper. She's never seen one."

"Then let's do it together." Mom took the box to the kitchen, and we followed. She put it on the island and reached for her kitchen scissors. I wanted to rush her and help, but I knew better.

"Now we can use this to call Mr. Lafferty on the phone."

"But he's deaf. He can't hear the phone, and besides, you said he didn't talk." Piper stood next to me.

"You're right, but he can see, and this is a special telephone." By that time, Mom had the device out of the box, and I explained to Piper how it worked.

The doorbell rang again. It was Piper's mother, and they were in a hurry to leave. I followed her to the door to say goodbye. "Practice your fingerspelling. We can sign in class tomorrow."

Mrs. Hanson and Piper weren't even out of the driveway before Mom asked, "So, what's this you said about signing in class tomorrow? Is this a project I don't know about?"

I followed Mom back to the kitchen. "Not exactly."

She picked up the grater and started grating cheese again. "And what does that mean? It either is a project or it isn't."

"It isn't. It's just a new way we can communicate when we're at school." Mom could ask more questions than I did, only she got answers because I was required to give them to her.

"Wouldn't that be akin to writing notes in class? You've been in trouble for that before as I recall." Mom stirred the cheese into the pot of milk on the stove.

I saw the box of elbow macaroni. "Are you making macaroni and cheese, my favorite? You make it the best, Mom."

She kept stirring, ignoring my question. "So, let me make certain I understand this. You and Piper are learning sign language so you can communicate in class without making sounds, and no one else will know what you're saying?"

"Well, I guess we could do that, but it's probably not a good idea. The main reason I'm learning sign language is to talk with Mr. Lafferty." I got the plates out to set the table even before she asked me to.

"You're so right. Bad idea. Maybe I should alert Mrs. Grayson that you're learning sign language and ask her to make certain you're not using it inappropriately at school."

"No need to do that, Mom. No signing in class and no passing notes either." I pulled four napkins from the napkin holder to finish setting the table.

Jackson came through the back door. "We're home. Got to shower. What time are we eating?"

Mom looked at the kitchen clock. "In about a half an hour."

Dad followed Jackson. "Anybody home?"

I rushed around the table to Dad and hugged him. "It's here."

"Great. It's home? Haven't seen It in a while. I'll be glad to see It."

I always laughed at Dad's corny jokes whether they were funny or not. For an attorney who was always reading something into what people said, he could be big-time literal sometimes. "Yes, sir. Mom, It, and I are home."

Dad chuckled.

"No, silly, the TTY is here. We already opened it. So can we set it up?"

"Could I put down my briefcase and kiss your mom first?"

"Oh, yes, the important stuff. That always comes first." My dad was still crazy about my mom. If I ever decided to get married, I wanted to marry someone like my dad. Jackson needed to take lessons from him. He had no clue about girls.

Dad kissed Mom's cheek and turned to check out the TTY on the kitchen island. He thumbed through the directions and picked up the device. "This shouldn't be so difficult. I think all it needs is power and a phone jack. Let me change clothes, and we'll set it up in my office. See if your mom needs any more help with the table while you wait, will you?"

Only a few minutes passed before the table was set and Dad had cleared a place on his desk for the TTY. Two plugs, and it was working. "Could I—I mean, could we—call Mr. Lafferty?" I stood over Dad's shoulder.

Dad pulled out his calendar. "Yes, in fact, I need to call him about bringing Mr. Hornsby out tomorrow." He looked at his watch. "But it's dinnertime. Let's eat and give Mr. Lafferty time to have his own meal. Then we'll check this thing out to see if it works."

"Okay." I stepped away from his chair. "I figured something out."

"Do tell. Will what you figured out make us rich?"

"No, sir. I was thinking about how to communicate with Mr. Lafferty since I don't know much sign language yet and Mrs. Walker won't be there to interpret. I was thinking if I used your laptop computer, I could just type what I can't sign. I can type pretty good now. Or if I had my own laptop computer, then I wouldn't have to use yours."

Dad put his arm around me, and we walked toward the kitchen. "I think that is ingenious. I'm so glad to have such a smart daughter who likes to figure things out, especially things involving my laptop computer. And, you know, I figured something important out too, when I started to represent Mr. Lafferty. There's a thing called a yellow legal pad, and then there's a pencil. They work really well, and Mr. Lafferty is accustomed to that."

"I guess that means no?" I saw Mom carrying two glasses of water to the table and grabbed the other two.

"It means I'll bring you a legal pad from the office. And besides, I have a feeling you'll be signing in no time."

After dinner, when I finished my chores, Dad and I went back to his office. "Could I call Mr. Lafferty and type the first message?"

Dad sat down in his chair. "Okay, let me get his number and dial it, then you can say the first hello." He dialed the number and slid the phone across his desk so I could reach it. It was no time before letters lit up and moved across the screen. *Hello, this is HL2. Who's calling, please?*

I responded slowly. I needed to learn the keyboard better. *It's Julia Russell. We have a TTY at home now. This is our first call. Now I can call you whenever I want to.*

Hi, Julia. How are you?

84

Fine, thank you, sir, and you?

Fine. How was school?

I learned quickly not to use so many words, and Mr. Lafferty didn't use many either. *Life Science and English fun. Math not so much.*

Math not good for me. Reading better.

Me too. See you tomorrow. My dad's bringing me.

Good.

Okay. Here's my dad. I'll be calling again, HL2. I got up and started out of the room. Dad moved to his chair and said, "Wait just a minute, Julia. I'll be done here shortly."

I looked out the window while Dad typed his messages. That spotted, stray dog was back. Jackson kept feeding him, so he'd never leave. I thought about Mr. Lafferty in that big, silent house. He might like a dog. Maybe he'd had one when he was a boy. I was glad he had a TTY. It was like his voice and his ears. Words had sounds, and they could be typed on the screen. I wondered about musical sounds and if there was a way for him to see them. What would it look like to Mr. Lafferty?

I was trying to figure that out when Dad said, "Julia, sit down."

"Is this another powwow?"

"A short one. First, I want you to know I'm very proud of you for wanting to befriend Mr. Lafferty. He needs friends, but we need to talk about some boundaries." Dad stretched back in his chair. "You must remember Mr. Lafferty doesn't see very many people, and he hasn't for many, many years."

"I know. Grancie told me all about it."

"She told you his story about when he was a boy, but I don't know how much she told you about how he lives now. He only sees Mrs. Schumacher and Mrs. Walker and me. He sees his doctor on occasion, but he mainly keeps to himself, and he hasn't left Emerald Crest in decades. I think we should be sensitive and not overwhelm him. And he's certainly never been around children before."

"Yes, he has. He went to that special school, and he was around children. And Grancie said he liked it there but couldn't stay after his mother died."

"That's true, but that's when he was a child. He's nearly sixty years old now, and he's been in that house since he was your age. So he's not been around children as an adult."

"Does he watch television? They have captioned programming now, you know."

Dad shook his head. "How do you know so much about so much, Julia? Yes, he watches TV. Mrs. Schumacher got all that set up for him a few years ago. I'd say he watches a few programs that interest him, but I think he reads mostly."

"Then he knows about how people act out there in the world. And he probably sees children on television."

"So do I, and they scare me. I can only imagine what Mr. Lafferty thinks."

"I don't scare him, except when I hug him. I think he likes me. He's like G-Pa, only not quite as old."

"You're correct. But like I said, let's be sensitive and not frighten him. And tomorrow I'm taking Mr. Hornsby out to meet him, and that'll be a big change. Let's just take things slowly. And about this TTY—you mustn't become a nuisance calling him whenever you have a whim. You are to always ask me before you call him. Understood?"

"Yes, sir. Understood. What time are we going tomorrow?"

"Four o'clock. I need to show Mr. Hornsby around the property before dark. You can stay with Mr. Lafferty while I do that. Take your sign language book."

"Yes, sir. May I go now?"

"To Mars, Jupiter, or to your room?"

"Is it okay if I have a whim to go to the kitchen for a cookie and milk? I didn't have dessert."

"In that case, I think I have a whim too. Lead the way. Take me to your cookies."

Mom didn't come in this time when she dropped me off at Dad's office. She knew we would be leaving for Emerald Crest soon. Mr. Hornsby was already seated in the lobby. Mrs. Mason offered me an apple for a snack. It was sitting on her desk like it was waiting for me. I was couldn't-stand-lunch-today hungry, so I took the apple and wished for peanut butter. "Could I have some coffee, Mrs. Mason?"

"You know, Julia, I poured your dad the last cup a few minutes ago, and I'm closing up the office just after you leave. Maybe next time."

Dad came out, and we were on our way. He started telling Mr. Hornsby about his job responsibilities. I opened my sign language book and practiced, but I was listening to every word. Dad was giving Mr. Hornsby the scoop.

"I was a bit concerned with the first window, but when the rock came through his second-floor bedroom window last week, I sensed someone was up to some mischief. I think it's time Mr. Lafferty had a foreman for the property. The house sits on the highest point right in the middle of a couple hundred acres. I've never walked the entire property, but I think it's time someone knows this property and what's going on out there."

"Yes, sir. I can get to know the land, and I'll do Mr. Lafferty a good job, a mighty fine job. And I tell you, I really appreciate the work."

I couldn't tell how old adults were because they all looked old to me, but Mr. Hornsby looked a little older than Dad. Mr. Lafferty would like him because he was wearing a red plaid flannel shirt and a plaid wool cap. His curly red hair was turning gray around the edges, and he had a beard. It was darker red, almost brown. He was tall and could have passed for a lumberjack if he hadn't been so skinny.

Dad said, "I don't think anyone means any harm to him. Probably just someone taunting him."

"That sounds about right. I've heard stories all my life about that old green mansion and the feller that lives up there and about the graveyard on the property. Even heard some of the boys when I was growin' up tellin' stories about goin' out there and snoopin' around. Probably just boys like that playing a prank or checking out them caves out there."

"That's a reasonable conclusion. You're aware that Mr. Lafferty is deaf and he uses a wheelchair?"

"No, sir. I did not know that. So how am I supposed to talk to him?"

"No need to talk. He's usually upstairs in his room by dark."

"I'll be sure to show up by then."

"Oh, I think if you're there by eight o'clock, that will be fine. Does that give you time to have supper with your family?"

"Yes, sir. But I'll be here all the time if you need me." Mr. Hornsby smiled big like he was very happy.

"I have an all-terrain vehicle coming next week. Until then, you can use my pickup truck to ride the roads that are cut. When we finish here, I'll take you to my house to get it. And you'll be using Mr. Lafferty's studio for an office and a place to stay warm. There's a bathroom and a small kitchen. He works out there sometimes in the daytime, but he comes back into the main house before sundown. He's a wood carver, you know, and a mighty fine one."

"I'll be looking forward to meetin' this gentleman."

"I'll introduce you to him, but I warn you that he's not used to having folks around, and I had to sell him hard on this idea. So let's just go slow." Dad looked back at me.

"I will do that. I'll go as slow as the smoke out of my chimney, but I'll be right 'ere iffen and when he needs me."

"When you get there in the evenings, all you need to do is turn the lights on and off out in the studio a couple of times. He can see it from his bedroom window, and he'll know you're there. And if he needs you, he'll do the same. It may take me a few weeks to talk him into giving you a key to the main house."

"I understand, Mr. Russell. That gentleman don't know me from Adam's house cat, but I'll take care of him. And he can trust me, sir. I'm just grateful to have this work."

"And we're grateful for you, Mr. Hornsby. What I'm hoping is that Mr. Lafferty will take to you, and he will want to hire you as the foreman for his property. I'm certain there are some jobs that need doing, some fencing repair and who knows what else."

"Yes, sir. About the only thing I can't do is electrical work. You have to go to school for that, but ever'thing else is right up my alley, and I do like to fix things."

"Let's just hope all this works out, and you may have yourself a full-time job. But you do understand I can't promise you that right now?" Dad stopped and used his remote to open the gate, then turned into the lane that would take us up to the house.

"I understand, sir." Mr. Hornsby turned around to look out the rearview window. "You do know that gate's useless, don't ya, Mr. Russell?" He took off his cap and scratched his head. "There's no fence on either side. But it's a mighty fine gate."

"I think it was something Mrs. Lafferty wanted. And you're right. It's mighty fine, impressive, and probably expensive, but most definitely a useless gate. Never even thought about it. And why don't you call me Ben, and I'd like to just call you Edgar, if that's okay with you."

"My oldest boy's named Ben. I'll be rememberin' your name. He's fine just like you. Then I have twin boys and a girl after them. They're good children, all doin' good in school, and my wife takes good care of 'em." Mr. Hornsby leaned forward in his seat as Dad parked in the driveway. "That's a big green house. Can't see it that good from the road, but it's green just like 'em stories I heard."

"It's green all right—green granite from somewhere up north, and green marble from Ireland. They built the outside walls out of the granite and the floors out of the green marble, and what's not green is mahogany wood. The Laffertys were from Ireland, and Mr. Lafferty the First wanted a house to match the color of his wife's dark-green eyes."

"She musta been a beauty."

Dad opened his door and then mine. "They say she was. Let's go meet Mr. Lafferty."

I rang the bell, the lights flickered, and Mrs. Schumacher answered the door. Dad introduced Mr. Hornsby to her, and she told us Mr. Lafferty was in the library and asked us to follow her. She led us down a long hallway across the entrance hall from the dining room where Mr. Lafferty usually met us.

I had never been down this hall, but if I was coming to see Mr. Lafferty every week, I thought I needed to learn to find my way around his house. That would be like the biggest treasure hunt ever. Just like in the dining room and the garden room, there were birds hanging on the walls down this hall.

Mrs. Schumacher motioned for us to enter a big doorway. I stopped to look around. I just kept looking up from the green floor to the blue ceiling. More bookshelves and books than the Sycamore Hill library. There were two ladders because the shelves were so tall. And more windows. I could see the garden.

Mr. Lafferty sat at a big table in the middle of the room. He had books spread out across the top. Dad introduced Mr. Hornsby, and all he got was a nod from Mr. Lafferty.

Then Dad spoke, and Mrs. Schumacher signed. "Mr. Hornsby is starting work tonight, and he understands about the lights in the studio when he arrives and that you will notify him the same way if you need him. He'll be using my truck until the other vehicle arrives."

Mr. Lafferty nodded again.

Dad finished, "If it's all right with you, I'll show Edgar around the property on the outside, and I'll leave Julia here with you."

Mr. Lafferty nodded and smiled this time. Dad and Mr. Hornsby left the room.

I signed *Hi* and his sign name to Mr. Lafferty. He waved back and motioned for me to come to the table. I walked nearer and stood next to him. All the books were opened to pictures about birds, and he pointed to them one by one. Then he went over to one of the bookshelves and pointed to a book on a shelf he couldn't reach. He fingerspelled the name of the book.

I wrote down the letters on the legal pad Dad gave me and signed *Yes* to let him know I understood. I climbed two steps on the ladder and got the book for him, but when I handed it to him, he wouldn't take it. He pointed to me and then signed *Home*.

I signed *Thank you*, and he followed with *You're welcome*.

It was a beginner book on carving. I began to thumb through it, but he touched my arm and motioned for me to follow him. He wheeled back over to the desk and opened a long drawer and pulled out a rolled-up bundle of something in a dark-brown cloth. He reached across the table and handed it to me, pointing to himself, extending his open palms to me, and then pointing to me.

I understood. He was giving this bundle to me.

Then he signed the letter *J.* His eyes asked me if I understood.

I signed *Yes.*

Then Mr. Lafferty signed the letter *J* again and touched his cheek with his little finger. It was almost like he used his little finger to pull the corner of his lip into a smile, and he smiled big.

I must have looked confused. So he put his right hand on his chest and then signed his name. Then he pointed to me and signed the *J* again, put his finger to his cheek, and smiled. Then it came to me: he was giving me my sign name. I didn't know much yet, but I knew when a person who is deaf gave a hearing person a sign name, it was important.

I heard Mrs. Schumacher behind me in the doorway. "Julia, he has given you a sign name. It means you make him smile."

I pointed to him and signed his name. Then I pointed to myself and signed mine.

Mr. Lafferty signed *Yes* and laughed. I laughed too. I was only almost eleven, but I knew this was one of those moments Grancie talked about, one of those moments that changed things. I knew this moment that Mr. Lafferty and I would always be friends.

Chapter Seven

G-PA PICKED ME UP FROM school on Friday for a sleepover. Grancie and I would be making iced pumpkin cookies and crocheting. If I was to finish my project in time, she and I would have our laps full of yarn right after supper. She was making prayer shawls for the nursing-home residents in Elkins, and I was making an afghan for Mom—a special one for Christmas with only red and green squares. She went crazy for Christmas, decorating and cooking, and she would go Mom-crazy that I'd made an afghan for her.

I had the wood-carving instruction book and the bundle H had given to me in my backpack. I couldn't wait to show it to G-Pa the minute I got to their house. I put my backpack in the chair at the breakfast table and unzipped it. "You know I'm learning sign language and Mr. Lafferty is teaching me about bird carving, don't you? Look what he gave me." I showed them the book first. Then I took the brown bundle and un-rolled it on the kitchen table. It had twelve pockets, each one holding a different tool. There was also a pocket with a stone in it. "These are carving tools, a whole set. I'm going back to his house next Tuesday afternoon for my sign language and bird-carving lessons."

Grancie looked at the carving tools. No use for words or signs from her. Her eyes said it all. The only knife she would allow me to use at her house wouldn't cut hot butter, and now I had my own set of gouging tools. I had read all about them.

G-Pa picked up one of the tools. "Oh, this is one fine instrument, Julia. The best." He rolled it in his hand and touched the blade with his index finger. "Sharp, really sharp. This is high-quality steel right here, and the handle looks like birch. Smooth, probably from Henry's hands. He must have spent hours using these."

"Do you really think they were his?" I picked up the stone. "And look, I think this is a diamond stone to sharpen the gouges." I handed it to G-Pa.

"Oh, I think they were his tools, and just look at the stone. I would imagine he spent about as much time keeping his tools sharp as he did carving wood." He put the tool and the stone away. "Once you can use these with some precision, he'll be introducing you to mallets and draw knives."

Grancie threw up her hands. "Oh my! Maybe you could just paint the birds he carves. Or you could just stick to your crochet needle. It won't cut."

"Henry's careful, Nancie. Remember his hands are more important to him than ours are to us."

I rolled the bundle back up and put it away. No more talk about carving gouges and draw knives. I didn't want Grancie asking my dad what he'd been thinking when he said yes to this. I knew what would distract her. "A rematch on Mexican Train? I won last time."

"Right after we get the cookies made. I have everything ready."

"Your famous recipe?"

"Oh, yes, the one my mother made. When the leaves start turning, it's time for those pumpkin cookies."

Grancie measured sugar and flour, and I sifted and added the spices. She showed me how to stir in the pumpkin. The house smelled so good. But the best part was drizzling the icing on the cookies after they cooled. Grancie made the best cookies in Sycamore Hill, and she was teaching me how to bake them.

When the last one was iced, I asked again, "A rematch on Mexican Train?"

"Dinner's done. I suppose you need a break before the crocheting starts." Grancie cleared the breakfast table. "How many cookies did you eat, Julia?"

"Only one." That was true. I had also licked the spoon with the icing a lot, but she didn't ask me about that.

"Well, if you only ate one, what about some caramel corn for our snack?"

"Homemade?" Grancie's was the best.

"Is there any other kind?"

G-Pa came into the kitchen and grabbed a cookie. "Did I hear somebody mention caramel corn and dominoes? Mexican Train has to be more fun than tangling yarn for hours, and I'm feeling lucky." G-Pa got up and headed for the drawer where they kept the dominoes.

While we played and ate caramel corn, I showed them the sign name Mr. Lafferty had given me.

"Now that's something, Julia," G-Pa said. "You can't decide your own sign name. A person who is deaf must give it to you. When Henry was an adolescent he gave me my name too—the letter *J* for John and then two pats of his palms together." G-Pa showed me his name. "That was the sign for *paper*. I think young Henry saw me and his grandfather always dealing with documents, and it just seemed to fit."

I stretched to add my domino to the train. "I read about sign names having meaning. Mrs. Schumacher said I made Mr. Lafferty smile. That's why he gave me my sign name."

"I'm glad you're making Henry smile. He hasn't had much to smile about in a very long time. Grancie told you about his mother. And then his grandmother Colleen did the best she could, learning how to sign and getting Henry out of the house. She even tried to put him in school in Sycamore Hill and agreed to pay extra for a teacher, but that didn't work out."

"So how did he get to be so smart?" I saw Grancie adding doubles to the train.

"He had a good command of language, and he could read before his mother died. So Colleen taught him at home. It was easier. Oh, they took him from here to New York and even to Europe to see if anything could be done about his hips and legs. He wasn't paralyzed, but the bones in his legs were crushed when the car hit him. They could probably fix that now, but not back then. And back then there weren't so many places where you could use a wheelchair. A few bad experiences left Henry convinced people were making fun of him, so he refused to leave the house. He felt safer there."

"I see what you mean about how he didn't have much to smile about."

Grancie had been quietly but steadily getting rid of her dominoes. "And then that grandfather of his. He wasn't nearly as loving as Colleen. He never learned to sign and pretty much ignored Henry."

G-Pa defended him. "Now, Nancie. I think he did the best he knew how. He was a man accustomed to building things and making things happen, and he couldn't fix Henry. He didn't know what to do. He provided a home and the best he could. I'm sure it pained him to know that he could do nothing else."

"He should have done better by that boy. Money doesn't do everything." Grancie had that scowl on her face like when Kiki, her spoiled dog, whined. "But he never learned to sign. And that left Henry in a totally silent house all alone when Colleen died."

I hadn't heard about his grandmother's dying. "How old was Henry when she died?"

G-Pa answered, "I think he was sixteen or seventeen, just

a young man. Colleen got pneumonia and died unexpectedly. And honestly, I don't think Mr. Lafferty ever got over her death. That woman was his life and his joy. They're buried side by side in a beautiful spot on the property right next to Mackenzie." He looked at Grancie. "Yep, Henry loved Colleen like I love you, Mrs. Russell."

Grancie smiled at him, and he winked. They were weird like that. G-Pa was a flirt, and Grancie loved it.

She said, "I shouldn't be so harsh on Mr. Lafferty. He did hire Mrs. Schumacher fairly soon after Colleen died. He brought her from Washington, DC, because she could sign. She was to take care of the house, cook, and assist when Henry needed assistance. And she's been there ever since. She's a wonderful, loyal woman."

"Yes, she is. Been there almost forty years, thanks to Henry Lafferty the First. She lived there for a while until she met a fine young man and got married. But Mr. Lafferty made certain she would be well cared for even after his death—that is, as long as she took good care of young Henry. She's like family." G-Pa stacked up some dominoes to make room for the train.

"I like her. She makes good hot tea and scones."

Grancie chuckled. "Sweetie, you'd like anyone who allowed you to have coffee or a cup of hot tea. You're a rare child."

"Yes, you are. You know you were born forty, don't you? But a cute forty with those blue eyes and curls of yours." G-Pa looked over his glasses at me.

"I had to be born forty because I think Jackson will be fourteen the rest of his life, and Mom and Dad don't need that."

Grancie laughed. "Well, I'm glad you're becoming Henry's friend. He must be comfortable with you. And don't you think it quite amazing that he has such a generous and kind spirit? All of his troubles could have made him a bitter, angry man, but they just seemed to make him better. In his silence, he must have learned some important lessons about living and making a difference in the world."

G-Pa looked over at me again. "Do you know who Confucius was?"

"You mean the ancient Chinese philosopher?"

G-Pa shook his head. "Born forty with an encyclopedia in your brain. Yes, that Confucius. Well, maybe you should know what he says about silence. I think it says something about Henry. Confucius said, 'Silence is the friend who never betrays.'"

"Hmm. That's a good one. I need to write that down and think about it. Maybe I'll tell it to Mr. Lafferty."

Grancie won the game. G-Pa and I talked too much and didn't pay attention. After dinner, we crocheted and watched a movie while G-Pa had a nice nap before bedtime, which came early at their house.

Grancie followed me upstairs to tuck me in. She called my room upstairs The Princess Room. "Julia, get that flannel gown on, girl, and let's pray. Anything you need to ask forgiveness for first?" She smiled.

Sometimes I thought she had antennae tuned in to what I was thinking and doing. I put on my gown and folded my clothes over the back of the chair. "I probably need to think about that, but when I think of something, I'll be sure to talk to God about it." She pulled the covers back, and I crawled in. "Is it ever okay to lie, Grancie? I mean, like if you know you're going to tell this really little-bitty fib to keep down trouble and you ask Jesus to forgive you ahead of time. That's okay, don't you think?"

Grancie sat down on the bed and pulled the covers up to my chin. "Well, that's a good question." She bowed her head like she was praying for an answer. "Hmm, it's not the best thing to lie, Julia. But I think what we're talking about is the greater good. So I think, on occasion, if it means really hurting someone's feelings if you tell the absolute truth and it doesn't hurt feelings if you don't, then maybe fibbing is the better thing to do. But I think it best to try to stay away from those situations when you can. When you start telling little-bitty fibs, as you call them, each one seems to get easier. And before long,

lying becomes the natural thing to do, and that's never good."
Then she touched her index finger to the tip of my nose. "We
don't want any noses growing around here. But I guess if you
find yourself needing to protect someone's feelings or to avoid
more trouble, then it's best to seriously think about what you're
doing first. And you might find it's better to ask Jesus what to
do than expect him to bless your fib and asking forgiveness
before you do it."

"Thanks, Grancie, I'll be thinking about that too.
Goodnight."

"Goodnight, sweet girl, and sweet dreams."

I sighed and snuggled down. I loved that big old bed in
my princess room. Grancie always had old, soft quilts and down
comforters for cold nights. But everything at her house was
comfortable.

The streetlight on the corner was shining through the window. We didn't have streetlights at our house. When we turned
out the lights, it was dark unless the moon was full, and it was
quiet—no cars, just night sounds. I thought about H living
in the quiet all the time. Maybe Confucius was right. Silence
was H's friend, and I thought he must be just as comfortable
surrounded with silence as I was wrapped in Grancie's quilt.

It was a good sleep. G-Pa woke me because Grancie was jug-
gling pots and pans to make my favorite Saturday-morning
breakfast: French toast with real maple syrup, scrambled eggs,
and two bacon strips. The frying bacon smelled like it did when
we went camping and Dad cooked breakfast over a campfire.

But then I smelled the coffee. G-Pa liked coffee made in
an old-fashioned percolator, and it was percolating really loud
this morning like it was in pain. I don't know which smelled
the best: the coffee or the bacon. I asked if I could have a cup
of coffee with three sugars.

G-Pa didn't answer. He just opened the cabinet and asked

me which coffee mug was my favorite. He was like that. Dad said he spoiled me, but I didn't think so. I thought G-Pa had spent his whole life arguing in court, and since he'd retired, he talked a lot about what was really important in life. And arguing over a cup of coffee was just not that important to him.

"I choose the red one, my favorite color."

Grancie said, "I'm not surprised you like red. Most girls like pink or purple, but not my granddaughter." She looked over my head at G-Pa. "Now, that coffee's strong, not like she's used to, so more milk, John, and only two sugars."

"Grancie's right. We're eating French toast. When you're having maple syrup, your coffee tastes even better when it's not so sweet. Trust me. I've been drinking coffee a long time."

Breakfast was so good, and G-Pa was right about the coffee not needing so much sugar. When we finished, he got up from the table and walked out onto the back porch to check the temperature. "It's thirty-eight degrees out there this morning. It is mid-November, and the sun's gone south. I guess Old Man Winter is letting us know he's on his way, and he'll be bringing Christmas in here before we know it. I already heard you'll be crocheting again this morning. Would you ladies like a fire in the study?"

Grancie answered before I could. "Oh, yes. What a perfect morning! Cold wind blowing and rustling the sycamore leaves, my second cup of coffee in front of the fire, and my favorite granddaughter sitting beside me with a ball of yarn and a needle."

It didn't take long before the fire was crackling. Grancie sat in her chair next to the fireplace, and I got comfy on the sofa. We were crocheting away like lickety-split. G-Pa took his favorite chair with the morning newspaper after he brought in another armload of firewood.

"Grancie, I've lost count. How many more squares until I can put the afghan all together?"

"Get the basket, sweetie, and we'll count them."

I went out to the sunroom and got the basket. It was full of red and green. I dumped it out on the floor in front of Grancie and started counting. "I have six rows already put together. That's forty-eight squares." Then I counted the single squares. "And I have eleven green squares and twelve red squares. So that's seventy-one squares altogether."

Grancie examined the rows and my single squares. "It usually takes about eleven rows of eight squares to make an afghan like you want."

"So, that's eighty-eight, and I need to make seventeen more. It takes me about fifteen minutes to make one square. Four more hours and fifteen minutes of crocheting. I can do this. It'll be ready for Mom for Christmas."

G-Pa continued with his newspaper and said, "My ten-year-old granddaughter knows who Confucius is and she's a talking calculator."

"It's really not that hard."

He laughed.

Grancie sat back in her chair while I packed the rows and squares back into the basket and set it next to the sofa. "You know, if you were making a lap quilt, you'd be finished. That only takes forty-eight squares."

"My granddaughter is not one to take the easy way out. She knows what she wants to do, Nancie, and she's going after it."

"I'm a Russell, remember? That's what Russells do." I picked up my needle and started crocheting again. *Forty-eight squares and I already have seventy-one. I need to think about this. I might have another plan, but it hasn't hatched yet.*

It wasn't long before I was talking about H again. "Dad told me Mr. Lafferty helps a lot of people."

G-Pa put down his newspaper. "You know you're not supposed to talk about those things, don't you? That's Henry's private business."

"Yes, sir. But since you already know all about it, and I'm just itching to talk to somebody, I can talk to you."

Then G-Pa started talking just like Grancie had when she'd told me the stories of when H was a baby. "Henry Lafferty the Second is what you might call a wealthy recluse, and he's Sycamore Hill's benefactor. Do you know what that means?"

I stopped crocheting. "I know what a recluse is. I looked that up. But I'm not sure about *benefactor*. Does that mean he uses his money to do good things?"

G-Pa propped his legs up on the ottoman in front of him and stretched back. "A talking calculator and a walking dictionary too. That's exactly what *benefactor* means."

Then he told me how Mr. Lafferty had been like a Secret Santa all these years, helping poor people and doing things to make our little town better.

"Like what?" I asked. "How did he make the town better? He doesn't even go to town."

"Well, he built the new library, for starters. Or at least most of the money was his."

"He did? He could have just given them his library and built a building for it. He has more books than I've ever seen."

"Well, when Henry goes to heaven, that will probably happen, and they'll build a new wing for all his books."

Then Grancie added, "And don't forget, he bought the new organ for the Presbyterian church. Imagine a man like that. He can't even hear, but he bought an organ so other folks could enjoy the music. And he makes sure all three schools have an art teacher and a music teacher every year."

"But I don't get it. If he never leaves his house, how did he even know the town needed a library or the church needed an organ or that some poor family needed help?"

"Until I retired, I kept Henry informed about the needs of the community. And he reads the newspaper, every word. This isn't such a big town, and he knows more about the people here than you can imagine. He has this uncanny ability to remember names. He probably remembers the name of the first boy he gave a bicycle to for Christmas, and the first woman who got the medicine she needed because he paid for it. And he expected me to remember their names too, and check on those folks from time to time. But he never wanted them to know the help came from him."

"So Dad's right. His heart pumps goodness. He just sits up there thinking of what he can do next to help somebody."

G-Pa looked straight at me. "Pretty much. I imagine Henry has a lot of time to think because he's not so distracted by what other people hear. And then your dad and I have the great gift of being Henry's voice and his hands to help folks, especially the ones who need a blessing."

"And then Mr. Lafferty gives them a blessing?"

"That's right. He feels his life has been blessed with such wealth so that he can bless someone else. He always said, 'It's just money, and I don't need that much money. It's too much blessing for just me.'"

I stopped crocheting. "He can't walk, he can't hear or speak, he can't leave his house, and he feels blessed. That doesn't make sense."

Grancie spoke. "Oh, yes, it does. It makes perfect sense if you look at things the way Henry does. He doesn't dwell on what he doesn't have or what he can't do. Life's entirely too short to think about those things. It wastes precious time."

"What do you mean, Grancie?"

She put down her crocheting needle. "You're always asking questions, Julia, so let me ask you one: What good would it do if Mr. Lafferty only thought about his limitations? No, let me ask you two questions: If that's what he did, how much joy would be in his heart?"

I was quiet for a minute. "I get it. His whole life would be wasted, and he would never know about all the good things he could be doing. It's got to be so much fun to do what he does. I really get it."

G-Pa chimed in. "Things like building a community, and helping educate some kids around here, and carving birds, and making some poor folks' lives not quite so hard." G-Pa paused. "And like teaching a young girl sign language—a young girl who's going to make her mark on the world. And it's going to be a good mark. I'm counting on it, and I imagine Henry is too."

"I never thought about it that way. I'll do my best not to disappoint you and Mr. Lafferty. But it's a long time before I'll be grown up and can make much difference."

The room got quiet. Grancie crocheted and hummed. G-Pa, sitting by that warm fire, just drifted off for a nap.

I couldn't stop thinking about Mr. Lafferty. I imagined him perched up there on that hill in that big green mansion, looking down over the town and wondering what he could do next to bless someone, sort of like God did. Mom said God didn't push himself on us. He just waited patiently, and while he was waiting, he was doing his business, listening to all our prayers and taking care of all his creation. And then I pictured Mr. Lafferty out in his garden with a swarm of birds all around him. Dad said he learned to feed them when he was a small boy. He was there with food in his hands, just sitting patiently in the garden until the birds came to him. I imagined he waited a long time before the first bird fed from his hand.

I wondered why Mr. Lafferty would choose to live up there all by himself and never come into town or have any friends. It didn't take long to answer that question. Who was going to talk to him? He didn't use his voice, and people would just stare at him and wonder why he didn't talk. He was always opening his hands to the birds and to everybody else, and he never expected anything back. Well, that was when I decided: Mr. Lafferty had been giving to this town forever, and he gave me a book and some carving tools, and he was teaching me so much. I was going to do something for him.

I have seventy-one granny squares. Twenty-eight more would be ninety-six. Seven hours to crochet. I will find seven hours, and Mom and H will both get lap quilts for Christmas.

Chapter Eight

D AD TOOK ME OUT TO Mr. Lafferty's on Tuesday afternoon after school. Mr. Hornsby must have heard us
coming up the hill. He stood in the driveway, his red
hair still poking out from under his cap and his plaid flannel
shirt peeking out from under his jacket. "Hello there, Mr. Russell. It's a fine day for you to be out. Been wet and nasty, but it's
clearing up." He opened the car door for me. "And hello there
to you too. Julia, isn't it?"

"Yes, sir."

"Now, you be careful walking. These rocks are still wet,
and they're mighty slick."

"Thank you, sir."

Dad guided me to the porch. "It's early for you to be out
here, Edgar."

"Well, you wanted me to get to know the place, and I can't
do that in the dark. Been a'comin' in the afternoons and walkin'
and drivin' these hills. It won't take me long to learn ever' rock
and tree."

"I appreciate that, and Mr. Lafferty will too when I let him know." Dad took my hand. "Let's step inside out of the cold."

"Yes, sir."

Mr. Hornsby followed us to the front door. "I been goin' home about the time Mr. Lafferty comes in from the studio. I build him a fire in his bedroom first, and then I go have supper with my family and come back for the night."

Dad rang the bell, and the lights flickered. "Sounds like you're getting along just fine with Mr. Lafferty and with Mrs. Schumacher."

"Yes, sir. Mrs. Schumacher don't need to be haulin' wood and buildin' no fires. I'm a-tryin' to help her out a little too."

Mrs. Schumacher answered the door. "Welcome, Ben." And then she looked at me, smiled, and signed my name. "Come in out of the cold. Mr. Lafferty's in the library waiting. And Julia, he has a surprise for you."

We stood in the front hallway, and Mr. Hornsby took off his wool cap. "I'll be gettin' on with my rounds. Goin' over to that north ridge this afternoon while the sun's shinin' a bit. Been rainin' the last couple of days, and I couldn't get up there."

Dad set down his briefcase. "I'm assuming since you haven't called me, there's been no sign of anyone around."

"No, sir. No sign. But the last few days it's been so wet and cold, I don't think even a vandalizer wanted to be out."

"That's good news. The new vehicle should be delivered tomorrow, and that'll make it easier for you to get around, especially during the winter months."

"Yes, sir. Surely will. And I'll be gettin' your truck back to you."

"Don't worry. I'll take care of that." Dad shook Mr. Hornsby's hand.

"Best be off." Mr. Hornsby started to open the door.

Mrs. Schumacher stopped him. "I'm about to serve tea and biscuits. Wouldn't you have some first?"

"Oh, no, ma'am. Don't want to waste no daylight." He put his cap back on and opened the door.

"Yes. I understand. But stop by before you leave to go home for supper. I made extra biscuits for your family."

"Yes, ma'am. My kids surely enjoyed those cookies you sent Sunday."

Mrs. Schumacher smoothed her apron. "That makes me happy. I do all this baking, and it's so wonderful to have someone enjoy it."

Mr. Hornsby left to do his work.

I thought H's giving-goodness had rubbed off on Mrs. Schumacher.

"Tea, everyone?"

Dad answered, "If you're making it, I could never turn it down."

Then she looked at me. "Milk and three sugars, right?"

"Yes, ma'am, please." And I was pleased. At home I drank tea every morning out of a coffee mug, but not when Mrs. Schumacher served it. She used real china cups with green shamrocks on the side, and she always served it with a saucer and a baby spoon.

Mrs. Schumacher sent us down the hallway and then toddled off in the other direction toward the kitchen. Dad and I entered the library, and he went to the smaller table in the corner to get out his computer.

H was at the library table just like he'd been on my last visit. Only this time it was cleared of all the books except for two. And the table was covered in a thick cloth that looked like leather. Tools and two small blocks of wood were lined up in front of him. He waved, signed my name, and picked up a tool. His eyes asked me the question, and I understood.

I signed *Yes* and pulled my bundle of tools from my backpack and put them on the table.

H signed *How are you?*

Fine, and how are you?

He picked up a tool with his left hand and signed with his right. *Today.* He pointed to the tools on his table.

I understood. Today we were carving wood. *Yes, you teach sign today also?*

His eyes moved quickly, always darting around, and his face was so expressive. *Learn sign when working.*

I didn't know the last signs. *What that sign? I don't know.*

He fingerspelled so fast I didn't get it.

Last time, I'd known I needed to learn some sign that would slow him down. I looked it up in my book. *Slowly, please.*

He smiled. Then he signed so slowly I think Dad might have gotten it. *W-o-r-k.* He signed *working* again.

I understand. I really liked the sign for *understand* because it looked like what it said—the flick of my index finger against my thumb right in front of my eyes, like a lightbulb going off in my brain.

H had a yellow pad and pencil on the table just like Dad said. When I saw it, I pulled mine out of my backpack.

He started writing. *Last week, you said you learn from DVD. What is DVD?*

I worked on writing down an explanation. Dad, seeing that I was taking a long time, came to stand over my shoulder. After a minute of reading, he signed *Wait.* Going back to his things, he moved his computer to the library table and turned it on. Then he got out a CD from its paper sleeve, held it up, and fingerspelled *D-V-D.* He plugged it into his computer and showed it to H.

H's face showed he got it.

I signed *You have a computer?*

H shook his head. I looked at Dad, then wrote quickly on my pad. *You should have a computer. They're fun. And you already know how to type on the TTY. I will teach you to use the computer. We can email and chat like the TTY.*

He took his pencil, underlined the word *email,* and put a question mark above it.

I wrote *It's electronic mail, like writing a note on paper except you do it on the computer, and then you can send it to anyone with an email address.*

Email addresses took more explaining.

H was so excited, almost agitated. He signed *Yes, yes!* and fingerspelled *e–m–a–i–l*.

Dad wrote on my legal pad. *I'll see to it. You should have one in just a few days. Julia is good with computers. She'll be a great teacher.*

H smiled and patted my back while I gave Dad my why-didn't-you-already-think-of-this look.

By then Mrs. Schumacher was serving tea and biscuits with strawberry jam. H liked his tea like I did—lots of milk and three sugars. After tea, Dad moved to the corner desk near the window and set up his computer. He said he was staying because it was too far to drive back to the office and then back out to Emerald Crest. That was true, but I thought the real reason was he wanted to make certain I did not annoy H.

H asked if I'd brought the wood-carving book. I got it from my backpack. He must have known that book from cover to cover, because he turned to a certain page that had pictures of a glove and a thumb guard. He opened the drawer and handed me a leather glove for my left hand and a thumb guard. It was thick leather, and I slipped it on my thumb just like putting a thimble on my middle finger when I embroidered with Grancie.

I wondered how H knew I was right-handed, so I wrote down that question.

H signed *I watch you write*, and he snickered. He took in everything with his eyes. Looking at things that closely would probably eliminate lots of my questions. My dad would love that.

H picked up two small pieces of wood only about three inches long and not very thick. He handed me one and kept the other. He wrote notes explaining this was basswood, his favorite for carving, and that we would carve a feather. He chose a tool from his box, pointed to the same tool in my bundle, and we started to carve. He'd do a few strokes and then point to me, and I would copy what he did. This went on for almost an hour. With every whittling away, my piece of wood looked more and more like a feather.

H finally put down his feather and his tool, removed his

glove and thumb guard, and pointed to me. I did the same, then he pointed to his watch. I thought maybe he was getting tired and wanted me to leave. He held up his hands in front of me and started wiggling his fingers like he was playing the piano. He quickly wrote *Time to play the piano* and started pushing away from the table.

I quickly put my things away in my backpack and followed him to the garden room. He took his place in the curve of the piano, and I took the piano bench. I played my last year's recital pieces. I had never played them for him. He signed *Again, please.* I repeated them.

And then he signed something I didn't understand. I guess he read my face before I could ask him about the word, because he shaped his hand like the letter *C* and made a large half circle, then he fingerspelled *C-h-r-i-s-t-m-a-s* and pointed to me. Pointing to me became his sign for asking me to repeat any new sign I learned. I did.

Then H signed *Christmas* and moved his hands again like he was playing the piano. I was playing "Jingle Bells" by the time his hands touched the piano to feel the vibrations. *Someday I will ask him about his Christmas memories.* I just knew he remembered, because he knew these Christmas songs.

Dad entered the room with his coat on and his briefcase and my jacket and backpack. It was time to go. I looked out the window. The sun was almost behind the mountain. G-Pa was right about November being here. The days were getting shorter, and time with H went by so quickly.

H had his legal pad on his lap and his pencil behind his ear. He wrote *Next week. Finish feather and start computer DVD.*

I smiled. I wasn't sure how much H understood about the computer, but I would teach him. I signed *Yes, and thank you very much.*

I couldn't teach him to hug without hugging him, so I went to his wheelchair, leaned over, and put my arms around his neck. He just sat there and held on to his pad and pencil.

I stood up and waved goodbye and signed his name. Signing his name was like blowing a kiss—two fingers to my lips and then I moved them to my heart. His mother must have given him that name.

Dad and I were out the door and down the hill by the time the sun had slipped behind the mountain. He was quiet while he drove, and I leaned my head back and thought about carving a feather and the new words I'd learned and how H was teaching me. I was doing and learning at the same time. I finally broke the silence. "Dad, I think this computer will change H's life."

"What's this with calling him H? Why not Mr. Lafferty?"

"Because he's H to me."

"No, Julia, he is Mr. Lafferty to you. It is more respectful to speak of him as Mr. Lafferty."

"Yes, sir. I understand, and I'll be respectful. You can count on it, but in my heart, he's still H." H's father was Mr. Henry Lafferty the First, and calling him Mr. Lafferty fit. Henry Lafferty the Second, my friend and teacher, was more like his sign name, and he was H to me.

Grancie and G-Pa were at our house for dinner when Dad and I got home. I told them all about seeing Mr. Lafferty and carving the bird feather. H had kept the feather and my glove and thumb guard, so I had nothing new to show them.

All the conversation around the table was about the Russell men's outing this weekend—pheasant hunting up near Pennsylvania in the same lodge they'd been going to since Dad was Jackson's age. It was their tradition the weekend before Thanksgiving. G-Pa reported, "Weather's supposed to be good, only slightly colder that far north. But no snow, and we should have pheasant for Thanksgiving."

Sometimes we had pheasant for Thanksgiving dinner, but Grancie always had a turkey in the freezer just in case.

While the Russell men were off on their annual expedition, the Russell women always went to Elkins to start the Christmas shopping. When Mom mentioned shopping at the table, Dad said, "I have a list for you. I hope you can help me out. I hate to ask since I know how much you hate to shop."

She smiled at Dad. "Oh, it will be such a burden, but I'll see what I can do." Mom had been born to shop. She always decorated the Christmas tree the Saturday after Thanksgiving, and she was not about to have the tree up with no presents underneath.

My grandparents didn't stay long after dinner. Grancie had calls to make about some project. I walked with them to the front door. When G-Pa opened it, a cold gust of wind blew inside. He pointed and said, "Wow, would you look at that beaver moon?"

I squeezed by him onto the porch to see. That moon could have been one of Grancie's white china plates hanging up in the sky. "Beaver moon. That's weird. Why do you call it that?"

G-Pa tugged on my curls. "Whoa, wait a minute! Something my talking-calculator and walking-dictionary of a granddaughter doesn't know?"

"That's right, but I'd like to know." I stood shivering on the porch.

"I'll mark this day on my calendar: the day I got to teach Julia something she didn't already know. Well, the Indians called the full moon in November the beaver moon because that was usually the last moon before the real freezing weather set in. It was when the beavers would be getting ready for the winter and a good time for the Indians to trap them before it got too cold and the water froze. Those Indians were hoping to get enough beaver skins to keep themselves warm until spring."

"That makes sense. So now I know about the beaver moon."

"Yes, you do, and don't forget it." G-Pa hugged me

goodnight, and Grancie kissed my cheek and said, "Run back inside and get warm, sweetie. Nothing will warm you like seasoned fir in the fireplace."

I did exactly that, and when I was warm, I had a glass of milk and went to my room to read for a while. Mom came up to say goodnight, and then the lights went out in the Russell house. The rain was gone, the sky was clear again, and that November beaver moon shone through my window, casting shadows through the bare limbs of the apple trees.

I remembered the conversation between Dad and Mrs. Schumacher that afternoon. She had given Dad a list. I didn't get it all, but I realized it was probably a list of what H wanted Dad to do for some families at Christmas. I wondered if that was the shopping Dad needed Mom to do.

I lay there thinking about giving H the Christmas lap quilt I was making. *Maybe he won't like it because he only likes plaid.* It wasn't much to give somebody who did so much to help other people. But what else was there I could do? I couldn't tell anybody about all the good things he'd done, and I couldn't buy him some expensive present. He wouldn't want that even if I could.

Grancie had always said life was short, and Mr. Lafferty never wasted time thinking about what he couldn't do. He just did all the things he *could* do. I didn't like wasting time either, so I'd better be figuring out what I *could* do instead of making a list of things I *couldn't* do. Christmas was coming. I had to do something special, and it couldn't be just a lap quilt made of red and green granny squares. Maybe if I went to sleep thinking about it, I'd have an answer tomorrow.

Friday came fast that week, and it was a cold morning. Mom served a big breakfast before Dad and Jackson packed up and left. I begged Mom to let me stay home since they'd allowed Jackson to miss a day of school to go hunting. She said no and took an unhappy me to school anyway.

I didn't know what grade I'd be in before we didn't study about the Pilgrims at Thanksgiving. I'd been doing that since kindergarten. At least we didn't have to make those cone-shaped hats out of construction paper and tape white buckles on our shoes.

We were fifth graders, and first thing that morning, Mrs. Grayson read to us about the Indians and the Pilgrims. I was tired of it and interrupted and told the class about the beaver moon. That was fact and a lot more interesting than one more made-up, hunky-dory story about the first Thanksgiving. Mrs. Grayson didn't seem very interested in knowing about trapping beavers.

I wanted to tell her that her story about the Pilgrims didn't tell the half of it and that the first Thanksgiving didn't look like the cartoon pictures in our textbook. Sure, the Pilgrims invited the Indians to celebrate their first harvest. But they probably ate fowl, which could have been sparrows instead of turkeys. And the Indians taught them to eat seafood, so lobster or oysters could have been on the table. And corn and green-bean casserole? No way. They probably ground what corn they had and made porridge with a little onion and salt. Teachers left out all the hard parts about the suffering and sickness and starvation. I guessed they thought children shouldn't know those things. But I'd read real stories about those times, and it was no fairy-tale feast with a big fat turkey on the table. So I zipped it shut. I wasn't about to spoil her story.

Mrs. Grayson kept us in for the morning break because of the cold and gave us twenty minutes of free time. Piper and I sat next to the window, and I told her about my visit to Emerald Crest and carving the bird feather and that I was crocheting a lap quilt for Mr. Lafferty.

She reported how one of the older girls in her dance troupe had hurt her ankle and she was having to learn her part because the girl wouldn't be ready for the Christmas theater performance. Then she said she'd heard Angus and Gary talking about the windows getting broken at the green haunted house.

"Did you tell them what I told you about the broken window?"

"No, I didn't tell anybody about that. You told me not to, and besides, you said it was just the wind. And for sure you know I don't talk to Angus. I just heard them talking during art class, and I didn't get much."

"Why didn't you tell me, Piper? I needed to know about that."

"We just had art two hours ago. This is our first break since then. I'm telling you now, Julia. It was nothing." Piper stood up and put her hand on the window. "It's really cold out there."

I moved beside her. "It can't be nothing, Piper. That's like a secret, a big secret. It's Mr. Lafferty's business. So how does Angus know?" I scanned the room. Angus and Gary were over by the terrarium looking at the toad.

"I don't know. Just go ask him."

"I'm going right now and do just that."

I bumped into the desk on my way around Piper. She grabbed the sleeve of my sweater. "No, Julia, you don't really want to talk to them. They're just stupid troublemakers."

"But they might know something, and I want to know what they know." I walked across the room to where Angus and Gary were. Angus was leaning over the terrarium, practically breathing on that poor toad.

"Angus." My throat was clogged, and he didn't hear me. I said it again. "Angus." This time it came out loud.

Angus raised up, bumped his head on the shelf, and turned around. "Yeah, what do you want?"

"What do you know about the broken window out at Emerald Crest?"

"I don't know nothing, and if I did, why should I tell you? I thought you knew everything about that old haunted, green house?"

Okay, Jesus, if you don't give me something to say real quick-like, I need you to forgive me for what I'm about to say. "I really don't know anything. I only said I did. I'm just curious, and you seem to have the most interesting stories about that old house and the man who lives there."

"Yeah, I know all about it—the house, the window, him, and everything."

I worked at being super interested. "Oh, tell me. Please, Angus. I like your stories."

"Somebody's been snooping around. Broke two windows trying to scare that mean old man that lives out there. Somebody's going to give him what's coming to him."

I had to cross my fingers behind my back and almost cross my eyes to say what I was about to say. "Must have been somebody really brave to go out to that scary old house."

"Yeah, it was. But they'll take care of business."

"Do you know who it was?"

He looked at Gary. "Yeah, I know. Gary does too."

"So, tell me, who was it?"

"Why do you want to know?"

By then the middle of my forehead was bound to be blood red. It was a Russell family trait when we got angry. My g-pa, my dad, and me. Jackson didn't have it because he didn't care about much of anything, so he didn't get mad often. "Angus, you'd better tell me who did that!"

Angus was smarter than I thought he was. He knew what I was doing. "Well, I ain't tellin', and I 'specially ain't tellin' you."

I screwed up my face at him and pushed my index finger right into his chest. "That's just fine. Don't tell me. But you're going to be real sorry because I'm finding out one way or another." I started to walk away but then turned around. "And Angus, keep your head out of that terrarium. Your breath's going to kill that poor frog." I stuck my tongue out at him.

Now what was I going to do? Dad was probably already at the hunting lodge with G-Pa and Jackson by now. He needed to know what I knew, but what could he do about it? And maybe it was nothing. Mr. Hornsby was there, looking after H. What I knew would just have to wait until Dad got home.

Chapter Nine

THE GUYS WERE GONE, AND it was girl's night at our house Friday night. Grancie came carrying her overnight bag and a hot Zito's pizza with extra cheese for Mom and green olives for me. She slipped me a brown paper bag when Mom wasn't looking. Then she hugged me and whispered in my ear. "Take it to your room. I thought you might need a ball of red yarn and your crocheting needle in case you want to crochet in your room." Grancie thought of most everything. It was like she knew I was giving a lap quilt to H, but I hadn't told her.

We ate pizza, drank root beer, and watched a movie. I was glad when *THE END* finally flashed across the screen. That meant ice cream, and I didn't even care if it was a cold night in November. "Extra pecans and one more squirt of the chocolate syrup, please."

Mom grinned. "Why not?" She spooned out more nuts and squeezed more chocolate on our ice cream.

We sat around the breakfast table scraping the last streak of deliciousness from our bowls and planned the next day in Elkins. I was right. Mrs. Schumacher had given Dad instructions about buying Christmas gifts all right. They were for the Hornsby children. Mom and Grancie made their list of items and guessed at sizes based on ages. Then they decided where we'd shop and where to have lunch. Grancie said we shouldn't miss the tea room with the bakery.

"I think Mrs. Schumacher likes Mr. Hornsby's family. She made them cookies last weekend, and she made biscuits for him to take home too."

Grancie agreed. "She's always liked doing things for people. Of course, she's always taken care of Emerald Crest and Henry. Except for Henry, she's been alone most of her life with no one else to take care of. She's been devoted to the Laffertys since she first met them."

I licked my spoon. "But I thought you said she married and moved out of the mansion."

"Oh, she did. But her husband was killed in an awful mining accident years ago when she was just a young woman. She never remarried, and she has no children."

Mom added, "She's lived alone in town in the little cottage on Poplar Street all these years, but Ben says she's thinking about selling her house and moving back to Emerald Crest in light of these recent incidents with the broken windows."

"That makes a lot of sense. Neither she nor Henry are getting any younger, and neither of them should be living alone. It'll probably be more convenient and less worrisome for both of them. Lord knows that house is big enough for the two of them and two or three more families."

I listened to every word, but I had to bite my tongue not to mention what Angus had said at school today about knowing who broke the windows. Mom and Grancie couldn't do one thing about it except worry. Mom would tell Dad when he called to say goodnight. Then he'd worry about it too. Then he'd tell G-Pa. A never-ending circle of worry, so I kept my mouth shut.

I took my bowl to the sink. "Mrs. Schumacher told Dad

and me she was grateful to have someone eat all the things she bakes. I think she just likes giving things away like Mr. Lafferty does. She probably talked him into buying Christmas presents for the Hornsby family."

Grancie joined me at the sink. "Maybe so. Henry gets the pleasure of paying for the gifts and surprising that family, but we get the joy of doing all the shopping."

I looked up at Grancie. "Shopping's more fun when you spend somebody else's money, especially when all the money you have in the world is in a cubby hole in your desk."

"Ah, that's where you keep it?" Mom rinsed the dishes and put them in the dishwasher. "Best we get to bed. We'll get an early start. Let's say breakfast at seven thirty and on the road by eight thirty. And dress warmly in the morning, Julia. We'll be in and out of the cold most of the day tomorrow."

"Yes, ma'am." I gave goodnight hugs and climbed the stairs. I made two more red granny squares before my eyelids got too heavy to stay open.

It had been a long day, but the shopping was done. It was almost dark at five thirty these days, and Mom wanted to be home before then, but Grancie convinced her to stop for a bag of burgers on our way through Sycamore Hill. We pulled into the garage just as the stars began to twinkle. It took three of us and three trips back to the car to bring all the shopping bags into the family room.

Grancie said, "Glad we decided to buy the gift-wrapping paper at the bookstore. Saved us some time, and now we can get busy tonight right after we make these burgers and fries disappear."

Mom arranged the bags in the corner. "Great planning. That'll give us a head start on Christmas. We'll have gifts under our tree this time next Saturday, and you and your dad can take the Hornsbys' gifts out to Emerald Crest next Tuesday, Julia."

I didn't answer.

Mom said, "Julia, you've been quieter than usual all day today. I thought you'd have more fun shopping. Are you feeling all right?"

"Yes, ma'am. I feel just fine."

Grancie came over and brushed my curls away from my eyes. "I noticed that too. I thought the cup of coffee in the mall midafternoon would perk you up."

"I didn't really need perking up. Besides, my latte was mostly milk."

They don't know I know about Angus and the broken windows, and they don't know what I've been thinking about all day long.

We ate our hamburgers and the leftover pastries from our lunch at the bakery. Then the wrapping started. Mom cleared the kitchen island and got out all the supplies. "Let's wrap the Hornsbys' gifts first. Then we can box those up and put them away."

Grancie agreed. My job was to peel off the price tags. That was painful and almost impossible, like removing a freckle with a fingernail. Maybe if the shopkeepers had to remove the tags they'd find a better way. Mom wrapped and Grancie did ribbons.

Mom said, "Julia, we need to put some name tags on each gift, but we don't know the children's names unless you know them from school."

"No, ma'am. The only one I know is Ben. He's in sixth grade. I don't know the names of the little ones."

"Then go get a pad of sticky notes off your dad's desk. We'll describe the gift on the sticky note, and Mrs. Schumacher can find out their names later."

I went to Dad's office and found a sticky note pad. There it was—the TTY. I had been thinking about H all day and wanted to call to see if he was all right, but I'd promised Dad I would always ask him first. Dad wasn't at home. But a promise was a promise. I turned my head so I couldn't see the TTY and

120

went straight back to wrapping detail in the kitchen with my sticky note pad.

We finally finished. At least I'd thought we were finished. That was before Mom got out the glue gun and sent me for the bag of silk holly she'd bought. It wasn't enough to have a ribbon and a big bow. Grancie cut the holly into small sprigs, and Mom glued stems of holly into the ribbon somehow. Mom knew most of us would tear into those presents like our lives depended on it and would probably never even see the holly, but it was important to her. She liked pretty packages.

With the last one finished, the Hornsbys' gifts were stacked in pasteboard boxes in the mudroom. The gifts for friends and family were stuffed in the laundry room waiting for the tree decorating next week.

Mom put away the wrapping materials. "Hot chocolate, anyone?"

I was the first to say yes. "Right now, that sounds even better than last night's ice cream." Mom made real hot chocolate with milk and cocoa powder and a sprinkle of cinnamon. "I think we should send the Russell guys away more often. It's like we're on vacation when they're gone."

We got cozy in the family room with our warm mugs. Grancie propped up her feet. "No seasoned fir in the fireplace tonight, but it feels oh so good to sit down." She reached for the throw and put it across her legs.

I couldn't wait any longer. "I've been thinking."

Mom blotted her lips with her napkin. "Well, that's a surprise. So that's why you've been quiet all day?"

"Sort of. I can't think and talk at the same time, at least not about the things that were on my mind today."

"Sounds like some serious thinking."

"It was the shopping and thinking about what Christmas will be like around here for our family. And that made me think about what Christmas is like for people like the Hornsbys and Mr. Lafferty. Our family's small, but we're all right here together for Christmas Eve at your house after the church service, Grancie. And then everyone is at our house for all of Christmas Day. Aunt Helen and her family come from Pittsburgh every year. And we have traditions about food and going to church and opening presents and making music and telling stories and the Christmas jigsaw puzzle. So many things we do, and we're all happy, every one of us."

Grancie said, "We are that. This family knows how to have fun. We know what Christmas is all about: God changing human history forever and giving us something to be joyful about every day, and especially on Christmas."

Jesus, I know I usually ask you to forgive me, but not now. Thank you. Thank you for what Grancie said. Grancie had no idea, but she'd just said the thing I needed her to say—a perfect setup. "So, with all this joy we have around here, what if we could spread some of it to someone else this year? To someone who doesn't have much joy every day like we do."

Mom set her mug of hot chocolate on the table beside her. "I know exactly what you're thinking, Julia Avery Russell, daughter of mine."

I hated it when Mom said my whole name. It was a reminder of my initials. What had she been thinking? I could never in my whole life, until I got married, put my initials on anything. Jackson already called me Jarhead.

"You're thinking we should invite Mr. Lafferty here for Christmas."

"No, ma'am, I am not. But that's not a bad idea if my idea doesn't work."

"So, tell me. What's your idea?" As tired as they were, Mom and Grancie were curious and sat up straighter in their chairs and looked interested.

"Lately I've been hearing all kinds of stories about the good things Mr. Lafferty has been doing for this town all his life, not just at Christmas. And I don't think he's had a real

Christmas since his grandmother died. And Grancie, you told me about the fancy Christmas parties they had at Emerald Crest. I know he remembers because he still remembers the Christmas songs I play for him."

Grancie answered, "Oh, they had no big Christmas parties after Henry was born, so he wouldn't be remembering those. But I imagine Colleen made that place magical for him at Christmas. We could see the outside lights from the road, and I have a feeling it shimmered just as much on the inside. And like I told you, his mother and grandmother played the piano, and he would remember that."

Then Mom said, "Your dad still gets someone to hang lights from the trees outside, and Ben said Mrs. Schumacher puts up a small tree every year. Just so you know, Julia, we have invited Mr. Lafferty to come to our house for Christmas several times, and Grancie and G-Pa invited him for years as well, but he doesn't want to leave Emerald Crest."

"That's because he's afraid, Mom, and that's mostly what I've been thinking about. You know what you said, Grancie, about not wasting time thinking about things you can't do? Well, we know we *can't* get him out of his house for Christmas. So, what we *can* do is … we can take Christmas to him."

That got Grancie's attention. "You mean give up our family traditions and have our family Christmas at Emerald Crest? And we would all go out there for Christmas dinner?"

"Not exactly. I mean take a Christmas party to him. We should do something for him to make him feel like he belongs to the community and show the community he's a kind man, just a little different, but not like the stories the kids make up about him. He built the library, and he's never seen it. He's helped people that he's never met."

Mom moved to the edge of her chair. "Are you talking about inviting all those people to Mr. Lafferty's house?"

"No, ma'am. That would be just about the whole town. I

know that mansion is almost big enough, but all those people would send Mr. Lafferty into doing wheelies straight out the back door to his studio."

Mom asked, "If not the whole town, then who's coming to the party?"

"I was thinking about our kid's choir from church. That's only about twelve, and we fit in the church van. Mrs. Wilson always takes us to sing at the hospital, and we go caroling, and we do the Christmas play at church. But what if the children could go and sing for Mr. Lafferty? And maybe some of the parents would go with us and take cookies and hot chocolate like a party. And we could all take him presents."

"Oh, I don't know, Julia. It's really a sweet idea, but we would have to convince your dad that it would work and not cause hard feelings. He would not want this to be upsetting to Mr. Lafferty. And we don't know how he would react." Mom sat back in her chair, and Grancie didn't say a word.

"He deserves a party and presents, Mom. The presents don't have to be expensive ones—just something that we could make for him. He keeps giving and giving, and nobody gives him anything."

"But he likes it that way. No one knows he's the one who gives, and we can never tell his secret."

"We won't, and we don't really have to take presents. I've already thought about it. Nobody will know his secret. We'll only go out and sing a few songs for him. But then he would know people cared about him. All he knows is keeping secrets and living like a recluse because people were mean to him a long time ago. He might like people who were kind to him. And if we could take a bunch of people out there and they could meet him, then they'd stop telling those awful stories about the mean old man or the ghost that lives in that haunted green mansion. They need to know the truth. At least part of the truth." I didn't want to stop and give Mom a chance to say no, but I ran out of things to say.

Grancie sat like a silent statue in her chair with her feet

propped on the ottoman, but Mom sat on the edge of her chair, just about to start her hand-wringing routine. That was what she did before she said no. "It sounds sort of good, Julia, but do you have any idea how many ways this could go all wrong? I envision everything from unruly children to broken expensive pieces of art to cups of spilled punch and mud tracked through the house and—"

Grancie interrupted. "I love it. We should do it because we don't know how many ways it could go *right*. Something like this could be a changing moment in Henry Lafferty's life. Obviously, he's fond of Julia. He invited her to come out every week. And he has such respect for John and Ben. And now Mrs. Schumacher is thinking about moving back in, and Edgar Hornsby is out there every day. I think Henry is opening his door a bit, and we should just walk right through it with a big, happy Christmas party. If planned just right, this could be all kinds of wonderful."

When Grancie said that, I could have hugged her so hard she'd have trouble breathing. She was not a glass-half-empty kind of woman. Dad always said Grancie could look at an empty glass, think it was beautiful, and say, "Oh my, what an opportunity to fill the whole thing with whatever we'd like."

"We could make it wonderful, couldn't we?"

Mom answered, "I'm not so certain. And do we have time to get these plans together, Nancie? We have Thanksgiving and the hospital gala and so many other things on the calendar."

I stood up. "I could do it. I don't have all that stuff. I don't even have a calendar. I just have school."

Grancie chimed in. "And I'll help. Julia, you and Mrs. Wilson could be responsible for the program, and I'll be responsible for all the Christmas goodies. We can do this, Jennifer. You clear it with Ben, and I'll help if you need me. Julia, you clear it with Mrs. Wilson, and you might get your mom to be in on that conversation, and I'll do the rest. I just need to know how many will be going."

I was just about jumping up and down. "I can see it now.

The choir can sing; I can play the piano; Piper can do one of her Christmas ballet dances; and we can even do a play in sign language."

With that, Mom started the hand-wringing. "Julia, you only have three or four weeks. Let's just stick with the music. We know nothing about plays in sign language."

"Then I'll write one, a simple one, and I'll get Mrs. Walker to come and teach us. She'll do it because she likes Mr. Lafferty."

Sunday morning was even colder than Saturday. I thought I was the first one up. I had a big job to do today. I had to convince Mrs. Wilson that visiting Emerald Crest and singing for Mr. Lafferty was a good idea, and I couldn't even tell her all the reasons it was the right thing to do.

I squirmed through church, and I spotted Mrs. Wilson on the second row of the choir. I told Mom we needed to make a beeline for the choir room as soon as the pastor said amen. No way was Mrs. Wilson getting away before hearing me out.

When the pastor mentioned Thanksgiving and the first Pilgrims, I just zoned out. I already knew more than I wanted to know about Pilgrims and Indians and roasted turkeys. But when I heard him mention the word *courage* and how many ways it took courage to do what the early settlers did—leaving their families, sailing across an ocean on a ship without a motor, landing on foreign soil with nowhere to live, and making friends of hostile neighbors—then I listened. Now that was real. None of that made-up cartoon stuff. Being grateful for the people who came before us and what they did made more sense to me. That took real courage.

And I needed courage if my plan was going to work.

Mom and I spoke with Mrs. Wilson, and she listened when Mom told her about my idea. Not only did she agree, she said she had been thinking and praying about a different kind of project for the choir this Christmas, and this was the answer to her prayer. She put it on her calendar for Sunday afternoon, December twenty-third, at five o'clock.

"I must confess, Mrs. Wilson, this was all Julia's idea. We'll take care of all the arrangements if you just have the choir ready. Julia is determined to do a short program in sign language. I suppose we'll just have to see if she can make that work."

Mrs. Wilson played with the curls resting on my shoulder. "Oh, I just imagine Julia already has it all figured out. Count on me to help."

Mom spoke up. "Oh, you must understand that this may not happen. I need to check with my husband about Mr. Lafferty first. And then if it's a go, you can tell no one about it, and I mean no one. It will be a complete surprise, so we need to give some thought as to how we can keep this under wraps until the very day we go. I already have some ideas, but we can talk later after I see what Ben says."

"I understand. I penciled it on the calendar, and I'll wait to hear from you before I send out a note to the parents about the importance of rehearsals for a big surprise. They'll love it. Christmas is all about surprises."

Yes. The first big checkmark off the list. We joined Grancie in the car and told her the good news. She said, "It was just meant to be."

Grancie went home after lunch, and I told Mom I would be in my room for the afternoon, working on the Christmas play. The house would be quiet until Dad and Jackson got home later. Quiet time to think.

In exactly five Sundays, we would be surprising H with his first-ever Christmas party with new friends. My mind was a muddled mess of things I needed to do. Grancie always said a list kept her on track, so I sat at my desk and started one that included Piper, Mrs. Walker, and writing a play. Then I looked through a couple of my books to get ideas about writing plays. I wasn't so sure I could do that.

Reading made me sleepy, so I napped for a while. When I woke, I got up and moved my slipper chair over to the window overlooking the fruit trees and took my crocheting out of the brown paper bag. I thought looking out the window and crocheting might help me think of something good. I had crocheted so many granny squares already I didn't even need to look. My fingers knew what to do.

The view from my window said winter was coming—gray skies, brown grass, leafless apple tree limbs, and no more apples. I glanced out the window, especially when a bird flew by, and I crocheted, and I thought. Looking, crocheting, and thinking, all swirling around and around in my head like Piper's gerbil on his wheel, going nowhere fast.

Nothing came to me that would make me flick my index finger against my thumb at my forehead, like the lightbulb came on and I got it. That was until the sun went down behind the mountain in the distance. It looked like a halo on top of the peak. And that's when it came to me—a mountain surrounded with light. I knew how to write this play.

Mrs. Schumacher comes through the garden room just as I answer my phone. She stands waiting.

"Oh, hi, Dad," I say, trying to hold my excitement.

"You remember how you would shine my shoes when you were younger just because I did something extra nice for you?"

"Yes, sir, I do remember."

"Well, my shoes will be shining for this gala. I found what you're looking for, and I got my shoes dirty doing it, crawling around in the back side of that shed."

"You're serious? I can't believe it. It's been in the shed out back all this time?"

"Yes. Jackson helped me get it into the truck, and we'll be out there within the half hour."

"Great! I'll let Mr. Hornsby know you and Jackson are bringing it. And Piper? Well, she'll be beyond excited. You're the best. I'll check this off my list, and thanks so much. Oh, and I'll get on the shoe shining this evening. Love you."

Mrs. Schumacher smiles as I end the call. "Surely not the mountain?"

"Yes, ma'am, the mountain."

"That's good. Henry would like you to come up as soon as you can take a break—something about one detail for the gala."

"On my way." I practically skip up the steps to H's room. He's as full of questions as I am. Maybe that's another reason we became friends.

He may ask me thirteen questions, but he's not about to allow me to see what he's working on until he's good and ready.

Chapter Ten

I STOPPED WORKING ON MY play and went downstairs when I saw Dad's truck coming up the driveway. I made myself a peanut butter sandwich and listened to the report of their trip, what they saw, and what they brought home. They planned to dress the pheasants out back while still in their hunting clothes. I wondered whoever decided to call it "dressing" pheasants. Seemed more like it would be undressing them to me.

G-Pa asked Mom for two large pans, her chef's knife, and her strongest kitchen shears. He handed Jackson the shears and said, "Son, you killed some of them, you'll be eating them, and it's time now you learned how to dress them." When I heard him explaining to Jackson about using the shears to cut off wings and how he had to be careful of the sharp bones, and then how he'd have to cut off the legs and clip the skin in a certain place to peel it off the bird, I looked long at that peanut butter sandwich.

"The smell might get to you the first time, but it'll pass. Now, when you cut the bird's head off, you just run your finger down in his neck to remove the crop. Real hunters cut the crop open to examine it for the bird's last meal. Could be kernels of corn or seed or even grain. That tells them where the bird's been feeding, and that's the best hunting ground. Come on, boys, we have pheasants to dress."

That's when I wrapped the peanut butter sandwich up, put it in the fridge, and headed straight back upstairs. Mom asked, "Julia, don't you want your sandwich?"

"Not anymore. I'm going back to my room to work on the play."

"I'll call you later. We'll have a bowl of soup and our Sunday-night treat: popcorn."

There was a slight chance I could eat a bowl of soup later, but there was no—and I mean *no*—chance I'd put a kernel of popcorn in my mouth tonight. And I might end up a vegetarian before Thursday.

I sat at my desk, twirled my pencil, and looked at my story idea. I liked it, and I could see it. It was a good Christmas story, and I thought H would like it, but my play had big problems. Three boys and nine girls in the choir, and two of the boys didn't sing. They just mostly stood there hoping whatever we were doing would soon be over. Not enough time to learn and rehearse lots of lines, no way to build a set and take it, and nobody knew sign language. But Grancie had said not to waste time on *can'ts*.

So, what can *I do to fix the can'ts?*

The Russell hunters were out back at the shed, making so much noise the neighbors down the road could probably hear them. I glanced out the window. It was almost dark, but I could see the light on outside the shed. How could they be laughing and carrying on while doing what they were doing to those poor birds? I wished I had earplugs so I didn't have to hear them.

Wait a minute … I didn't need to hear them to imagine what they were doing. G-Pa had already put a picture of that in my brain. That was like Mr. Lafferty. He didn't need to hear to know what was going on if I gave him the picture. That's when it came to me. Mime. Why didn't I already think of that? Mime eliminated two huge *can'ts*. No one had to learn lines or sign language. And Piper would be so great at helping with mime because it was a lot like dance.

I started writing the simple story on my yellow legal pad. One person could read it while Mrs. Walker interpreted, and the rest of us would be mimes. Piper could do one dance, and we could learn the signs and sing "Go, Tell It on the Mountain." That would be it. It didn't have to be long. But the story had to be something, really something. H had to get it—the story and the story behind the story. That was the most important part.

I came down early the next morning for breakfast. Mom stirred the oatmeal and then started buttering the English muffins. I whispered to her, "I finished my play. I figured it all out. I just hope Mr. Lafferty will like it." I looked around to see if Dad was coming in. "Did you ask Dad last night? What did he say?"

"I did. We talked, and I'll let him give you his decision."

It wasn't long before we were all around the table and Dad was praying. I thought I couldn't wait. I was scared to ask. It was like being in the courtroom when the jury's decision was already made, and I was waiting to hear but not sure if I wanted to know. Finally, Dad spoke. "Julia, your mom says you came up with an idea about a Christmas party."

"Yes, sir. And Grancie wants to, and Mrs. Wilson said yes, and I've already written the Christmas play. And it's really good."

"Um-huh. No need to plead your case. I've already made my decision."

I put my spoon down and raised my arms over my head. "So, can we take Mr. Lafferty a Christmas party and change his life and make him happy or not?"

"You certainly know how to phrase a question, daughter." Dad stirred his oatmeal. "And you did get right down to the heart of the matter, and that's Mr. Lafferty's pleasure."

"But Grancie said she thought it was time, that Mr. Lafferty had opened his door a little to me and Mr. Hornsby, and she thought we should march right in with a Christmas party."

"I can understand why Grancie thinks that."

"But what do you think? It's all up to you, Dad. Mr. Lafferty's whole Christmas is up to you."

"I'm thinking it might work, but I can't say yes until I have a conversation with Mrs. Schumacher. If this plan has a chance of working, we will need her help. And I think she's the one who will know best how Mr. Lafferty would respond."

"Yes!" I was so excited I spewed oatmeal. "So when will you talk to her?"

"I'll talk to her this week. But young lady, you'd better keep this quiet, and no talk of the confidential things you know."

"Yes, sir. I don't want to do anything to upset Mr. Lafferty. But I really, really, really think he's going to like this. Grancie said it could be the moment that could change the rest of his life."

Dad shook his head. "Grancie and her life-changing moments. She's been talking about those for as long as I can remember."

I wanted to tell Dad what Angus said, but this was no time to be bringing up broken windows at Emerald Crest. He could change his mind about the party. I hated knowing things I couldn't talk about. That list was getting longer. I hoped I could remember.

Dad dropped Jackson and me off at school. I knew it wasn't for sure we were having the Christmas party, but I told Piper about my ideas anyway. She liked my story and promised to help with the mime.

She and I were eating lunch together. I couldn't look at the niblet corn or the chicken, so I just ate the green beans and spice cake. Angus came by after he got his tray, looked squinty-eyed at me, and said, "Wouldn't you like to know, Julia?"

I wanted to knock his lunch tray out of his hand. "Know what, Angus? You're the one who doesn't know anything. And besides, I know all I need to know."

He stood there with Gary right beside him. "You know what I'm talking about. About who broke the windows out at that creepy green house."

Jesus, forgive me. I'm about to tell another fib, but it's for the greater good like Grancie said. "I don't care about that old house or any broken windows. Go choke on your chicken."

"Oh, you'd like to know, and it's going to happen again soon. I know that too."

My head buzzed, and my insides were churning like Mom's new spin-cycle washing machine. "Remember what I said, Angus. I know all I need to know. And I know you have stink breath."

"Yeah, and you have bird legs and bug eyes."

"Just go away, Angus, or I'll use one of these bird legs to kick you to the other end of this table."

Angus and Gary laughed and walked away and sat down. Piper grabbed my arm. Her face looked like it did when her gerbil crawled down her shirt. "Julia, what got into you? You shouldn't be saying that kind of stuff to Angus. He's mean, and he'll do payback. What did your dad say when you told him about Angus?"

"Remember, he was gone all weekend, and I didn't tell him yet."

"You didn't tell him? But he should know, especially if it's happening again."

"Maybe I'll tell him tonight. And I'll give him the new information. But it won't be happening again. Mr. Hornsby is looking out for Mr. Lafferty and Emerald Crest."

I told Dad everything Angus said that night when he got home from work. He didn't like it. When we got to Emerald Crest on Tuesday afternoon for my second bird-carving lesson, he reminded me he would talk to Mrs. Schumacher about the party. He sent me in and said he was going to the studio and would be back in a few minutes. I knew he was going to look for Mr. Hornsby. He'd be telling him what I learned from Angus and asking him to be on the lookout.

Mrs. Schumacher answered the door. "Welcome, Julia. You'll be seeing Mr. Lafferty in the library again today. He wanted to take you to the studio across the garden, but it's a bit cold, and Mr. Hornsby is out there speaking with an electrician."

"Yes, ma'am. Dad is on his way out there too. He said to tell you he'd be in shortly. He has something very important to ask you."

"Oh, he does, does he? While I'm waiting for that conversation, suppose I go and make a pot of tea, and I have some pound-cake cookies. Lots of milk and three sugars if I remember correctly?"

"Yes, thank you. Except for only two sugars if you have cookies. Coffee or tea is better not so sweet with sweets. And pound-cake cookies are my favorite. Grancie makes them too. She's famous for them."

Mrs. Schumacher stroked my hair. "Wise girl about the sugar, and I should ask your Grancie for her recipe. Maybe hers is better than mine since she's famous for them. Now scurry on down to the library. Mr. Lafferty's waiting on you."

H was seated at the big table in the library just like last week and the week before. He smiled and motioned for me to come in. I waved and set my backpack down in the chair at the end of the table, opened it, and pulled out my carving tools, my yellow legal pad, and a surprise for H—two tail feathers from one of the pheasants Dad had brought home.

He took the feathers and examined them and signed *Thank you.* I wrote a quick note telling him about the pheasant hunt. He replied in a few words that Dad usually brought pheasant to him at Thanksgiving, but he'd never brought the tail feathers. I wrote back explaining I thought he might like to see one since we were carving feathers.

Our unfinished feathers, gloves, and thumb guards were already out and in front of him. The books were open to the same pages. He pulled out a different tool, and I did the same. Last week we'd trimmed away the wood, leaving a piece the shape of a feather. This week the work would be more detailed. He didn't have to write that or sign it. He pointed to the book, picked up his tool, and started carving. I did the same.

H and I were learning to communicate, and it was like we had our own language. Sometimes he would stop and teach me a new sign. Other times he'd fingerspell or write a short note. And sometimes he looked at me and I just knew. Every time he taught me a new sign, I wrote down the word on my yellow pad so I could practice and remember.

We were carving away when Mrs. Schumacher served tea in the same china cups. H didn't want to stop working on the feather. He wanted me to eat my cookie and start back to work. Dad came in shortly after that. I heard him talking to Mrs. Schumacher over in the corner, but it wasn't about a party. He was asking something about outside lights, and everything about her said no, no, no. Dad disappeared and returned in a matter of minutes to open his computer and start to work at the corner desk.

H looked at the grandfather clock in the corner three times. I heard it chime every fifteen minutes. At exactly five o'clock, he brushed the wood shavings into a pile, removed his glove, and put away his feather. He reached for my feather and examined it, then signed *Good, good.* Then he taught me the signs for *smooth, balance,* and *important.*

I wanted to learn everything H would teach me. He was patient, and it seemed everything he did was with purpose.

He tapped on his watch and signed *piano*. I followed him into the garden room and played for him. Dad stayed in the library with Mrs. Schumacher. I could hardly play for thinking about the conversation they were having. I hoped that everything about her was not saying no, no, no to the Christmas party.

Dad was smiling when he came into the room. I could only pray that meant yes.

Before we left, H handed me a hymnbook from the bookshelf. He opened it to "Go, Tell It on the Mountain" and signed *You know* and drew a question mark in the air with his index finger.

My whole chest felt like a cage full of butterflies. That was the song I'd chosen for the play, and it must be H's favorite. *Jesus, forgive me, but I'm not about to spoil the surprise.* I signed *No*.

H closed the book and signed *You can learn*. He rolled across the room to the chair where my backpack was and put the book next to it.

It was time to go. I hugged him and signed *I will learn song*.

He smiled and followed us to the door.

Dad hadn't even turned the ignition key before I was asking, "What did Mrs. Schumacher say, Dad? Please don't make me wait any longer. I know she had to say yes."

"She said yes, and she thought it was a good idea. And she said, 'If anyone can make this okay with Mr. Lafferty, it will be Julia.'"

"It was a sign. I knew it." Then I explained to Dad how I had chosen "Go, Tell It on the Mountain" and how H had given me that very music to learn today. "This is great. Now we just start to work. Tomorrow is choir practice, and I'll take my story for Mrs. Wilson to read. Mom can talk to her too. I already have a list of costumes, and we only need one prop."

"Costumes, props? I'm not sure Mrs. Schumacher agreed to that. I told her we'd keep it very simple. How many people are we talking about, Julia? I told her about twenty or twenty-five."

"That sounds right, or maybe thirty-five."

Dad opened the gate with the remote. "But I thought

you'd just sing a couple of songs with the choir out in the garden room, and we could have refreshments in the dining room. We can't fit thirty-five people in the garden room."

"Is there another room?" This was getting complicated.

"There's a grand hall where they hosted parties decades ago, but I don't know when that room has been opened. It's one whole wing of the house."

"But we must have a piano. So we can't use that room."

"Who said it doesn't have a piano?"

Butterflies were again about to explode. "What? Nobody has two pianos."

Dad chuckled. "The Laffertys do, and the one in the grand hall is just like the one in the garden room, only bigger."

"What? And I'll bet it has ivory keys too." That was another big *can't* erased. "And that takes care of the room we need for one prop. We only need one." Another *can't* gone.

"Okay, Julia. You'd really better get this act together and make it work."

"I will, Dad. I was so afraid when I heard you and Mrs. Schumacher in the corner that she was saying no to the party. What was that all about?"

Dad explained his idea about installing motion detectors in light of the broken windows. "Mr. Hornsby and I met with an electrician this afternoon about the possibilities, but Mr. Hornsby thought it wasn't such a good idea. He said there are so many animals that could set off the lights, and Mr. Lafferty is so sensitive it just might be more trouble than it's worth. Don't know why I didn't think of that myself, and Mrs. Schumacher said no in a hurry."

"Sounds like Mr. Hornsby and Mr. Lafferty are getting along just fine. And I think Mr. Hornsby will take care of things."

"I asked him to be on the alert, and he will be."

"Did you give him the pheasants?"

"I did, and was he ever happy! I left one for Mrs. Schumacher to prepare for Thanksgiving dinner for them. And you'll be glad to know there were plenty of birds left for the Russell clan too."

"We're having pheasant for Thanksgiving?"

"Yes, we are, served on the turkey platter just like it might have been a gobbler. And your mom and Grancie are making all the trimmings."

Right. I would definitely be a vegetarian by then. No way I could swallow a bird that Jackson had skinned. I'd just be grateful for green beans and sweet potatoes. "We can tell Grancie tonight about the party. She'll be so happy that she'll start baking next Monday morning."

"You're probably right. Now, about that prop you need. You need mine and G-Pa's help with that? If you do, we might need to get started as soon as we get the house decorated and the Christmas lights strung outside."

I was grinning on the inside. "Yes, sir, but it won't be hard."

"What is it?"

My grin leaked out when I looked at Dad. "Just a mountain."

Chapter Eleven

THANKSGIVING DAY AT THE RUSSELL'S was a feast day starting with a breakfast casserole and Grancie's drop biscuits. The Russell men were in the woods hunting before sunup, came home for breakfast, and left again.

Grancie and Mom spent the morning in the kitchen baking pies and corn bread for the dressing, getting ready for our Thanksgiving meal, which was usually around two o'clock. This was the first year I'd gotten my very own job. Mom handed me the recipe and all the ingredients for the green-bean casserole. Then I was to peel oranges for the cranberry salad.

I usually set the table, but not today. Mom had outdone herself with burlap, acorns, gourds, pumpkins, dried hickory nuts, and some bare limbs from the red maple out back of the shed. Instead, I poured canned soup over the green beans and told Grancie about taking my Christmas story to choir rehearsal yesterday. "The play is a mime, a picture story for Mr. Lafferty. Piper and her mom said they'd teach us all the actions, but I have some of my own ideas about that since I wrote the play. I think Mrs. Wilson likes this plan because all she really has to do is teach our choir two stanzas of 'Go, Tell It on the Mountain.' She's planning to write a special letter to the parents inviting them to go with us to a surprise party. I think that's a great idea."

Mom chopped pecans. "We're talking a surprise party, all right. Usually surprise parties are just for one, but this party? It'll be a surprise for everyone." She sprinkled the last chopped nuts on top and put the pecan pie in the oven, then turned to Grancie. "Julia says I'm in charge of costumes, and I could use the help of your ladies in the sewing ministry at church."

"Oh, they'll be so happy to help. They're getting bored with making pajamas for the nursing-home patients. We just need a pattern or a description, and I'll be happy to supply all the fabric."

Mom swished by me with the dishrag in her hand. "Tell her what you need, Julia."

"Well, we only have two characters with special costumes, maybe three, but we don't have to worry about Piper. She has more costumes than Jackson has baseball cards. So that leaves the king. I see him dressed in white and gold, with a big crown and a long, white beard, sort of like God."

Grancie laughed at me. "Oh, so that's what you think God looks like. Walking around in heaven all day in flowing white robes and a crown on his head. I'm glad to know that."

"Not really. This king in my story is sort of like God. I know God doesn't look like us or wear a white robe or anything like that. But this king has to look special."

Grancie chopped celery for the cranberry salad. "Okay. A white robe with a gold sash, and we'll make him a gold crown to be remembered. In fact, we may already have one in the costume closet at the church. So, what else?"

"Then we need nine kids dressed in clothes like they wore when Jesus was on earth."

Grancie laughed. "Oh my. We are not using king-sized pillowcases or striped bathrobes with a rope belt, are we? I've seen too many costumes like that in my time."

"Maybe more like togas in blue, green, or gray, and the girls need something over their heads like a shawl. Rope belts are good, and we've got lots of rope in the shed. We could get Dad to cut it in the lengths we need. But we need one costume that's different ..." I stopped to think. "I think it should be dark purple and simple, but with a gold sash like the king. And that's all."

"Why, that'll be a piece of cake. We should be able to get that done in no time flat. And I'll talk with Mrs. Wilson about asking the parents to bring a Christmas treat. I think it would be best if everyone participated in the party." She turned to Mom. "Jennifer, maybe you and I should make the hot cider and a few extra goodies just to be sure it's festive like we want. And Julia, I'll call Mrs. Schumacher. That's a long overdue call anyway. I'll ask her about her plans for Christmas decorations. Why, I think this party is just about planned."

When I told Grancie about choosing the song and how Mr. Lafferty had given me the music Tuesday, she said again, "Like I told you. This party was meant to be."

"Grancie, you remember what you said about Mr. Lafferty doing what he can instead of complaining about what he can't do? We're turning all the *can'ts* into *cans*—everything from the play being a mime to performing in the big living room with a piano. It's all working out."

"That's amazing, Julia. Maybe we're getting a bit of divine help. What do you think?"

"I didn't think of it that way, that God would be too interested in a Christmas party. Lots more important things for him to think about. Besides, there'll be lots of other folks having Christmas parties around here ... and all around the world." Grancie frowned, and I added quickly, "But if God's interested in this one, then it will be the best Christmas surprise party ever. I can hardly wait."

Mom called Grancie over to the crockpot on the counter. She lifted the lid, and the smell of bacon mixed with garlic poured into the kitchen. "I wrapped the pheasants in bacon and put them on a bed of carrots, onions, celery, and a whole head of garlic and poured in a little wine. They've been cooking for over four hours. Do you think I should turn them off?"

"I think they're done enough. They'll stay warm, and we'll take off the bacon, brush them with a bit of butter and honey glaze, and put them under the broiler for a few minutes before we're ready to serve."

My mind was made up. They could wrap those pheasants up in honey and tie them with bacon strips like we wrap the Christmas presents and float them in whatever, but I wasn't touching anything that'd had feathers on it or Jackson's hand down its throat.

The morning passed. The hunters returned to clean up, and G-Pa left to pick up an elderly couple who had no family around and nowhere to be today. When he returned with his friends, we were ready to take our seats, and G-Pa said grace. Seemed there were always extra folks at our table for Easter and Thanksgiving, and there was enough talk that no one noticed I passed the pheasant to Mom without putting any on my plate.

After lunch, when the food was put away and G-Pa and Grancie left to take their friends home, I asked Dad if we could call Mr. Lafferty on the TTY. He resisted at first and suggested we call later. But when I reminded him the football game was coming on at four, he changed his tune. We went into his office. Dad dialed the number and let me type the message. It rang lots of times, and I was about to give up. But then H answered. *This is HL2.*

I quickly responded. *This is Julia. Happy Thanksgiving.*

Hi, same to you and to your family.

Finished our meal. I made green-bean casserole. Wish you could have been here.

Couldn't leave Mrs. Schumacher alone. Early dinner at five. But thank you.

I said I was thankful for my new friend, Mr. Henry Lafferty the Second, because he's teaching me sign language and how to carve birds.

Nicest message ever. Thank you for playing piano. Lovely memories. Pianos need playing. Grateful to be your friend.

You're welcome, Mr. Lafferty. My dad says hello from our family and not to bother you any longer. So, goodbye.

Goodbye. See you Tuesday.

If Mr. Lafferty only knew what I was planning … I hoped he would still be thankful I was his friend after December twenty-third.

Friday was dress-the-Russell's-house-for-Christmas day. Mom warned Dad and Jackson there'd be no leaving the house or games on television until the decorating was done. We morphed into the Russell brigade—Dad in the attic pulling out plastic bins of decorations and handing them to Jackson on the attic stairs, Jackson stacking them up in the garage, and Mom and me bringing them into the house. Mom had learned a long time ago about packing and labeling the boxes. She liked things organized.

The labels told us exactly where to put each bin. All artificial fruit to the dining room. All snow globes to the fireplace in the family room. Ceramic nativity, red ribbons, and garland to the entry hall. Wooden nativity to the hearth in the family room. Then came the box of framed family Christmas photos, which went to the kitchen. That was an odd place, but those framed photos were unpacked, unwrapped, and placed all over the house, even in the guest bathroom. Bins and boxes of Christmas tree decorations went into the corner of the family room awaiting the Christmas tree, which would arrive on Saturday.

When Christmas was out of the attic, the assignments started. Jackson and Dad had only to string the silk garland up the stairway and hang the big wreath on the front door. Mom checked their work and dismissed them. Then she began making things beautiful in the entry hall. She tied big red-velvet ribbons and attached them to the garland on the stairs. She cleared the big round table in the entry, spread a gold cloth over it, and assembled the nativity with one white pillar candle in the middle. I didn't think Mom understood much about mangers, or there'd be no gold cloth; she'd be scratching up some hay from the neighbor's barn. But she liked things neat and pretty. Once again I'd have to find another place for my backpack until January.

Then she went to the dining room. I helped her unpack handblown glass balls that she hung from the arms of the light fixture over the table. She removed everything from the antique sideboard and covered it in green velvet and sparkly fruit. She was careful to put the big pineapple in the center. She studied the colors and shapes and chose just the right place for the glittery apples, pears, oranges, lemons, bananas, and pomegranates. She worked to make them look like someone had just spilled them out of a bucket.

"I did this with real fruit and fresh greenery one year," she reminisced. "Oh, it was so beautiful and smelled so fresh, but by Christmas it was ruined and smelled like a garbage heap. And, honestly, it bothered me a bit that I wasted fruit when there are hungry people in the world. So, after Christmas that year, I bought all this artificial fruit on sale, and it looks lovely. Later we'll get your dad and Jackson to cut some fresh cedar for greenery to fill in around the fruit."

"That will make it smell so good."

Then Mom set the dining table just like we were having someone over for Christmas dinner that night. She had a Christmas tablecloth and napkins and special china just for Christmas. It was her mother's. She even put out the glasses. I lost count of the little crystal candleholders, and red candles sprinkled the length of the table.

Then she sent me looking for the bin of red and green satin Christmas balls. Jackson didn't read, so I knew where to look. It was sure to be in the family room with the tree decorations.

Mom put the satin balls in a big glass bowl in the middle of the table and then backed away to look. "Needs a bit of cedar stuck here and there, don't you think?"

"It's beautiful, Mom, but like I said, cedar will make it smell so good in here."

"Why, thank you, Julia. I do hope you're learning so that someday, when you're all grown up, you'll decorate your own house and make it lovely with all the things you love." Christmas was like the Thanksgiving Pilgrims. Somehow, after a few hundred years, the characters got all dressed up. Somebody cleaned them all up and put them in satin and velvet. I guessed we just didn't like to think about how rough it was, and how hard it was when Jesus was born.

The dining room was done except for the fresh greenery. Mom sent Dad and Jackson to cut cedar and hemlock. "Cut lots, now. I need it for the dining room and the mantel."

She asked me to unwrap the wooden nativity that always went on the hearth while she started unpacking the snow globes she had collected since she was a girl. She placed several on the mantel, and those that were left over she put all around the house with the family photos.

By the time the greenery was in buckets in the garage, snow globes lined the mantel, and the wooden manger scene was nestled on the hearth on leftover hay from last Christmas. Jackson and I had grown up playing with that set. It was safe and couldn't be broken—except for the donkey's tail, which Jackson had broken off years ago. Dad had glued it back on. Still, we'd be hearing a lot of "Jackson, be careful!" the next few weeks. Too many pretties around for a teenage boy who was mostly arms and legs and only a cupful of brains.

By the end of the day, everywhere I looked it said Christmas. Our house smelled like cedar and looked like something out of a magazine. The unpacked bins were stacked in the hallway. Dad breezed through the kitchen and asked, "Would you like us to get these back in the attic this afternoon?"

"If you'd like, or you could just stack them in the garage

until after we decorate the tree tomorrow. Then it can all be put away at one time."

Dad knew how to make Mom feel good, so he said, "Take a walk with me through the house, and show me everything you did." They walked out of the kitchen holding hands.

I wanted to follow, but somehow it didn't feel right. Instead, I went to the family room. Jackson was watching another ball game. I said, "Get up, Jackson, and do something. I need you to help me."

"You're not the boss of me, li'l sister. Besides, I'm doing something. I'm watching the game."

"Okay, be a slob. Mom's tired, and the bins have to be moved to the garage before she can fix dinner, but I'll do it by myself."

I stomped off, but to my surprise I had only carried one bin out when Jackson joined me. By the time Mom and Dad got back to the kitchen, the bins were stacked in the garage. Dad raised his eyebrows. "Wow, just like magic the bins are back in the attic."

I corrected him. "Not in the attic yet, just in the garage."

"Either way, it seems a shame to me to put Christmas in the attic. Your mom makes the house look so lovely at Christmas, and it's only one month out of the year. Then it's back to the attic for Christmas for another eleven months."

Mom slipped around behind Dad and hugged him. "No, sweetheart, only the Christmas decorations go to the attic. Christmas is with us every day." She kissed him on the cheek, walked to the sink, and washed her hands. "We ate Thanksgiving leftovers for lunch, and I'm too tired to cook. So, Ben, dinner is yours."

"Wonderful, let's take a vote. Zito's pizza or burgers and shakes?"

We all shouted our favorite.

"Oh, no, it's a tie, and I'm not going to both places. So, Jenn, you wanted pizza, and that's what we're having. I'll phone it in and pick it up."

I hugged Dad. "Extra cheese and green olives, please, and no Italian sausage."

Jackson flipped my hair off my shoulder. "But I like the Italian sausage. You're such a baby. You should try it. It's good."

"I can't even look at it since you said it looked like rabbit droppings."

Dad laughed. "I'll order two pizzas, and tomorrow morning we'll go cut our tree and get a bag of burgers for lunch. My treat."

Old Man Winter had blasted in by Saturday morning. It was our tradition to have waffles, eggs, and sausage at home and then make our annual trip up to Brushy Creek Tree Farm to cut down our Christmas tree. We bundled up and squeezed into Dad's truck. I had to sit in Mom's lap during the hour-long drive. Dad turned on the FM station that played only Christmas music from Halloween until January. We sang along for a while.

The owner of the tree farm met us like he always did and gave Dad a map. Mom liked Douglas firs, but Dad liked the blue spruce because it smelled so good. This was Dad's year to decide. After an hour of walking, looking, and sniffing trees, we had a truckload of a blue spruce, and I was bluer than the spruce from being so cold. I was the first one to climb into the truck.

"Turn on the heater in a hurry, Dad. My hands and feet are about to fall off."

Jackson laughed. "You should have had hand and feet warmers like me. My hands and feet are as warm as toast."

"What are hand and feet warmers?"

"This." Jackson pulled off his glove. In the palm of his hand sat a warm packet. "Got something similar in my shoes. We wear them hunting. Something you didn't know about."

"Thanks for sharing, Jackson." I put my hands up to the heater.

Perhaps it was the heat, or perhaps the excitement, but in

no time the cabin of the truck was toasty warm and we were all laughing and chattering and singing carols for the return trip. And then, after cheeseburgers and fries, it was tree trimming time. Dad and Jackson brought in the spruce and secured it in the corner. Mom popped popcorn and gave it to Jackson to string—a necessary job since he couldn't be trusted with anything breakable. She knew he would eat half of it, but it kept him busy.

Now, Mom had a thing about decorating, but Dad had a thing about Christmas music. He found his favorite Christmas CD, turned up the volume, and started unpacking the Christmas tree lights. That was his job and always first. Mom was organized about that, too, making certain the lights were not put away tangled. She helped Dad place them just right on the tree.

When there were no more strings of lights, Dad said, "Crawl under there, Julia, and plug them in, please."

I eased behind the tree, and Dad handed me the plug. "Okay, here goes. Everybody, hold your breath."

Yes. All the lights came on to a chorus of "Yeah!" and "Oooh!"

Mom unpacked the ornaments—the beautiful collectible ones that Jackson wasn't allowed to touch, the ones we'd made with popsicle sticks and glitter to frame a Christmas picture, the handmade stuffed ones Grancie had made, and the ones that were souvenirs from family vacations. It seemed every ornament had a story, and Mom and Dad liked telling those stories as they hung them on the tree.

I lifted a shoe box out of the bin. "What's this?"

Dad said, "Open it and see. I think you'll like them, but be careful."

I sat on the sofa and lifted the lid and a layer of bubble wrap. There were several small bundles of tissue paper. I unwrapped the first one. It was a hand-painted wooden cardinal. Mr. Lafferty. It had to be. "Did Mr. Lafferty give you this?"

"Yes, and every one of those in the box. I get a new one every year, and they're always cardinals."

I examined the detail. "This is beautiful, but he doesn't paint his birds."

Dad stopped what he was doing and sat down next to me. "He only paints cardinals."

Mom, the artist in the family, spoke up. "It's really more like staining them a deep red. Then he does some burnishing on the feathers for detail and paints the eyes, the beak, and the legs."

I unwrapped six of them, each one different, perched on twigs or in flight. "They're beautiful. Why haven't I seen these before?"

Mom answered, "I don't know. We hang them on the tree every year, but we never told you the story."

"Oh, could I have just one to put in my box of ornaments?" Mom and Grancie had started making and buying ornaments for Jackson and me ever since we were born. We had our own bins with our names on them, and we would get them when we moved out on our own.

Dad picked up a bird from the box. "You've seen the cardinals out at Emerald Crest, haven't you? They're Mr. Lafferty's favorite bird."

"But at his house, he always carves two together."

"There's a reason for that. G-Pa told me this story when I started getting these for Christmas. Mr. Lafferty gave him cardinals too. You remember Mr. Lafferty's mother was killed when he was just about your age?"

I nodded my head and kept looking at the cardinal, feeling the smoothness.

"Well, his grandmother told him to always think of his mother every time he saw a cardinal. His mother had red hair. I think he carves cardinals to remember his mother. And I think he carves the pair to remind him of his grandparents. They loved each other very much, and you know, cardinals mate for life."

"I like that story, Dad."

"Maybe one day I'll take you out to the grave sites for his family. They're buried out on a hill in a grove of chestnut oaks not far from the house. There are three large headstones with names and dates, and each one has an etched cardinal in the stone."

"I'd really like to see that. Has Mr. Lafferty ever been out there? I mean, can he get there in his wheelchair?"

"Oh, yes, there is a brick path from the garden to the burial place. He goes out there frequently and feeds the birds right out of his hand, mostly cardinals. It's very beautiful and peaceful there."

"I really want to go out there with him to see that."

Dad put his arm around me. "Maybe he'll take you one day, but you'd have to sit as still and quiet as he does to see the birds." Dad put the cardinal back in the box. "Choose the one you like, and you can put it in your bin of ornaments after Christmas."

I chose the one I wanted—the one in flight—and hung it on the front of the tree where I could see it all the time. I wanted to keep it in my room after Christmas, but I would ask about that later.

Mom said, "Okay, it's all done. Another beautiful Christmas tree. And, Ben, I really like the spruce. It does make this room smell good."

Dad went over to Mom and hugged and kissed her. "Don't need any mistletoe in this house."

She giggled. "It's time to put these boxes and bins in the attic. Hop to it, Jackson. You've been idle long enough."

Dad and Jackson were in the garage hauling bins back to the attic and Mom was cleaning up his popcorn mess when the phone rang. But it was a different ring than usual. I looked around for Dad's cell phone. Then I realized. The TTY.

I ran to Dad's office. The lights were blinking. I answered. *Hello, this is Julia.*

HL2. ANOTHER WINDOW. MR. HORNSBY CHASING TWO. TELL BEN TO COME WHEN HE CAN.

Chapter Twelve

H HUNG UP. I LOOKED at the clock. 6:38. I ran to the garage. "Dad, H just called." I forgot I wasn't supposed to call him that. "You must go, and you have to get there fast. He used all capital letters."

"What? Julia, slow down." Dad came down the attic stairs.

"It's another broken window, and Mr. Lafferty wants you to come right now."

"How do you know this?" Dad shuffled the rest of the bins out of the pathway to the mudroom. "Oh, yes, the TTY. I forgot."

"He just called. He said Mr. Hornsby was chasing two guys. He watched them from the window."

"Two. One is vandalism. Two? That's trouble." Dad looked at Mom. "Could you get me the key to the mansion? It's in my top right-hand desk drawer, and it's labeled." Then he looked at Jackson. "Son, get your heavy jacket. You're going with me."

"Yes, sir. I'll get the big flashlight from the gun closet. You want me to get my gun?"

"No. Don't need to shoot anybody over a broken window.

Just the light, and let's get going." Dad looked at me. "Did Mr. Lafferty say anything else?"

"No, sir, just to get there as soon as you can." I followed Dad inside. "I'm getting my jacket too."

"No, you're not. You're staying here with your mom." Dad grabbed his heavy coat and gloves.

"But Mr. Lafferty's my friend, and Jackson doesn't even know him. I can make him feel okay. And besides, you can't even communicate with him."

"Not happening, Julia. You'll be more help here talking to him on the TTY. Come on, Jackson."

Mom returned with the key. Dad and Jackson were in the truck and out of the garage in less than three minutes.

I stood in the driveway and watched the tail lights on the truck get smaller and smaller. I was no crybaby, but I felt like crying. I'd begged to go, but Dad refused. I was Mr. Lafferty's friend, but Jackson got to go. Jackson could throw a ball and run fast, but I was a girl, a smart girl, so I got to stay home. Not fair—nothing about it fair. I'd be a lot more help than Jackson.

Mom tried to make it okay, but I went inside and straight to the TTY and called H. He answered quickly. I typed *My dad and my brother on the way.*

He responded *Good. Still nothing from Edgar. I'm upstairs. Downstairs window in the breakfast room this time. Can see it from up here.*

I typed as fast as I could. *Stay upstairs. Dad has key to your house.*

Mr. Hornsby chasing on ATV. Watched him drive north of studio. Can't see lights now.

It's okay. Dad will be there in just a few minutes.

Hanging up, moving to another window. Will call back. H was gone.

Mom walked into the office. "Are you still on with Mr. Lafferty?"

"No, ma'am. He just hung up. He was going to another

window to try to see the lights from the ATV."

"Don't worry, Julia. Everything will be just fine. It's only a broken window. They'll get to the bottom of this, and meantime, Mr. Lafferty is safe." Mom walked over to the desk. "Why don't you come in the kitchen with me? You can help, and we'll have the soup ready when your dad and Jackson get back. And I'm putting some brownies in the oven."

"I can't do that, Mom. Mr. Lafferty said he would call back. Did Dad take his cell phone?"

"I don't know, but that's a good question. I'll go see."

I waited for Mr. Lafferty. I waited for Mom. And I thought. Just like Angus had said—it had happened again. I wondered what he knew. I looked at the clock. Two more minutes had gone by.

Mom called from the hallway. "Your dad must have his phone. I can't find it. It's not on the charger or on the dresser. I'll call him on my cell and see if he answers."

"If he does, tell him Mr. Hornsby is on the ATV and went north of the studio." I waited another few minutes that seemed like hours.

Mom returned to the office door. "Your dad answered, and I gave him the message. Jackson thought to get your dad's phone."

"Maybe Jackson has more than just one cupful of brains after all," I mumbled.

"What was that, Julia?"

Jesus, forgive me. "I was just being grateful for my big brother who used his head today."

I waited. I stared at the TTY screen. No use to call. Another six minutes passed. Then that strange ring and H's message. *HL2 again. Ben and Jackson here. Will drive around to find Mr. Hornsby.*

Dad has cell. Talked to Mom. I stand by to relay messages.

Good girl. Then things went silent. Fifteen more minutes, then Mom's cell rang.

She came to the office. "Is Mr. Lafferty on the line?"

"No, ma'am, but I can call him."

"Call him. Tell him there's been a minor accident. Your dad and Jackson found Mr. Hornsby. The ATV slid. He has a leg injury. They're bringing him back to the house."

I called H and gave him the message. Then more waiting. Finally, Dad called and told Mom what had happened.

Mom put her phone into her pocket. "Okay, Julia. Mr. Lafferty's fine. Your dad is taking Mr. Hornsby into town to get his leg checked out and some abrasions cleaned up. Nothing serious there. Jackson's cleaning up the downstairs area, and they'll board it up when your dad gets back. Mr. Hornsby will stay the night with Mr. Lafferty inside the mansion." She was counting things on her fingers so she wouldn't forget. "Four things. That's all, so, let's get to the kitchen and rustle up something warm for them to eat when they get home. It's cold, and there's been enough excitement for the night."

"But what if Mr. Lafferty calls?"

"Then you'll take the call, but I'm sure you can hear it in the kitchen. No need for you sitting here staring at the screen. Jackson is with Mr. Lafferty if he needs anything."

I followed Mom out of the office. She went through the family room, turned on some Christmas music, and lit the candles on the mantel. The fire Dad had built earlier was mostly embers, so she added some wood and stoked it. "I think we'll have our soup and sandwiches in here tonight. It's just too beautiful not to sit here and enjoy the fire and the lights."

I did all the things Mom asked, trying to pass the time. I asked lots of what-if questions, but she didn't really have any answers. Mr. Lafferty didn't call again.

Finally, Dad and Jackson got home. I looked at the clock. 9:37. Nearly three hours of worry. And why? *Because somebody's mean—just plain mean—enough to want to cause Mr. Lafferty more problems than he already has.*

We ate and then Dad gave us a full report of what he knew. "Seems Mr. Hornsby was upstairs to build a fire in

Phyllis Clark Nichols

Mr. Lafferty's bedroom when he heard the crash downstairs. He looked out the window and could see two figures with flashlights running from the kitchen wing across the garden and around the studio. When he got downstairs, he found the picture window in the breakfast room broken. He ran out, got on the ATV, and started in the direction in which he saw the two running. Since they had flashlights, he could chase them. When it's dark out there, it's really dark. So any light's easily spotted."

I was curious. "Did he get a good look at them?"

"No, just shapes, but he thought they were young fellows from their clothing."

"If he could see them and he was driving, why didn't he catch up with them?"

Jackson answered before Dad could. "Out there in the dark, running on foot's probably faster than driving that ATV."

"Doesn't it have headlights?"

Dad answered, "Yes, I had some put on."

"So, if he could see where he was going, how did he get hurt?"

"There's my girl with all the questions. Well, he chased the two guys down the lane, and then the fellows got smart. They left the path and started running through the rough country. Mr. Hornsby followed them into some thick woods and was going as fast as he could to keep up. He doesn't have much experience driving the ATV yet, especially under those circumstances. He lost sight of their flashlights and heard some hollering. So he stopped and turned off the ATV to try to hear them. There was nothing—no light and no sound. He assumed they got away. When he cranked the vehicle back up, he accelerated too quickly, lost control, and sideswiped a tree. At least the vehicle didn't flip, so he just has some bruises and scratches. His right ankle will be sore for a while, though."

Jackson piped up. "Yeah, I got to drive the ATV back to the house. I followed Dad in the truck."

"But they got away. Dad, I told you what Angus said. He

157

said it was going to happen again. That stupid stink-breath knows something."

Mom spoke up right away. "Julia Avery Russell. I do believe you need a new vocabulary list and a lesson in human kindness."

"But Mom, Angus is a troublemaker, and Gary just follows along."

"Those boys are not my responsibility, but you are. And we do not speak of others that way in this household. Do you understand?"

"Yes, ma'am."

Dad interrupted. "Well, Julia does have a point, not about the stupid stink-breath stuff, but Angus knows something." Dad got up with his plate. "I need to make a call."

Jackson followed him. "And I need to take a shower."

Mom tried to stop them. "But we have brownies, and I was about to make hot chocolate for dessert."

Dad spoke on his way out of the kitchen. "This won't take long. I'll be done by the time you get the hot chocolate made."

Jackson went upstairs for a shower, and I went to the kitchen to help Mom with the dishes. I was slicing brownies and putting them on the plate when Dad returned. "Ladies, best make one more cup of hot chocolate and an extra brownie. Officer Whitson is on his way over here."

I put the extra brownie on a plate. "Who's Officer Whitson?"

"He's an officer with the Sycamore Hill police department. I've never filed a report about the vandalism because Mr. Lafferty didn't want me to. But I think it's time. This must be stopped. And Julia, he'll be asking questions about your conversation with Angus."

"What I say could get Angus in a lot of trouble, couldn't it?"

"Maybe, if he's done something to get in trouble about."

"Dad, do you think Angus did this? And maybe Gary, because Gary would eat worms if Angus told him to."

"No. Edgar said these fellows were about Jackson's size. One was even bigger."

"Then it wasn't Angus. He's stocky for his age, but Gary's skinny like me, and probably no taller."

"Then whatever you say shouldn't get them in trouble. But I must tell you, Julia, after the officer hears what you have to say, he'll probably want to ask Angus some questions."

I didn't like it that I'd be labeled a snitch at school, but I didn't like it that somebody was causing trouble for Mr. Lafferty either. "I'll tell the officer everything I know, Dad."

Officer Whitson arrived just a few minutes later. Mom served him dessert with the family around the Christmas tree. Mom was just that way, always wanting to put a sugar coating on everything. I told the officer all I could remember that Angus had told me, even about knowing that another window was going to be broken soon. Between eating his brownie and sipping his hot chocolate, he made notes on a small pad he had taken out of his pocket just like officers did on television.

Jackson kept interrupting, telling the officer about cleaning up the glass and boarding up the window and then driving the ATV back to the house. He talked like he was a hero or something.

Finally, the officer nodded. He put his pad away, thanked me for being a brave girl, and thanked Mom for a warm dessert on such a cold night. He told Dad he would follow up in the next day or two, and Dad saw him out the front door.

Jackson had already left for his room by the time Dad came back in the family room and stood in front of the fire. "It's been a long day, ladies, and I'm dog tired. Why, we've cut down the most beautiful tree at Brushy Creek Tree Farm and decorated it today! Sunday morning will come early, and we have a big day at church tomorrow. I'm headed for the shower and my bed." Dad kissed me goodnight and left the room.

I said goodnight to Mom and went upstairs. No way I could sleep, and I wasn't about to waste good time. I grabbed the paper bag from under my bed and pulled out the yarn and needle and crocheted while I thought about why anybody would waste time being mean. That act had frightened Mr. Lafferty, made all kinds of problems for my dad, and caused Mr. Hornsby to get hurt. And now somebody was going to be found out and be in trouble.

One and a half granny squares later, I still hadn't figured it out, but I crammed the bag under my bed and closed my eyes.

Dad called to check on Mr. Lafferty Sunday morning. All was well. Mr. Hornsby had gone home, and Mrs. Schumacher was there for the day.

We went to Grancie's for Sunday lunch after church—Waldorf salad, a pot of beef stew, and her famous corn bread. I let go of my vegetarian routine since beef didn't have feathers.

After Grancie's carrot cake for dessert, G-Pa took Dad and Jackson to his office to show them a picture of a new gun he was thinking of buying. I helped clear the table, and when the kitchen was clean, the list-making started—lists of Christmas cookies they'd make for all the upcoming things on their calendars. They planned to do the baking together at Grancie's house. I heard her say most kitchens weren't big enough for two women, but hers was.

"Oh, you have to make your pound-cake cookies, Grancie. We can put red and green sprinkles on them, and Mrs. Schumacher would like your recipe. She makes them too, but they're not as good as yours."

"I'll be happy to share my recipe, and if you want pound-cake cookies for the party, you'll have to help me bake them."

We heard a phone ring twice, and it wasn't long before Dad and Jackson came to the kitchen. "Okay, ladies, the guys need to be gone for a while."

I could always tell when Grancie's antennae were up.

She looked Dad dead in the eyes. "What's going on, and where's John?"

"He's changing clothes. Officer Whitson just called and said we have two boys missing in the community and asked if we could join a search party."

Mom asked, "Do we know the boys, and what do you mean missing?"

"I don't know much right now, but apparently Derrick Smithson and Wendell Brady didn't come home last night. Their car's missing, and they think there might have been foul play."

Mom said, "I know those parents. They must be frightened out of their minds. Jackson, do you know those boys?"

"I know them from football, but they're varsity players, and I'm just junior varsity. They don't have much to do with us."

I had antennae like Grancie's, and right now they were waving fast and strong. "Dad, think about it. Two teenage boys missing, and it was two teenage boys that Mr. Lafferty and Mr. Hornsby saw last night. That's a heaping can full of coincidence, don't you think?"

G-Pa walked into the kitchen with his jacket. "Julia's right. Could be coincidence, but not likely."

"Twenty years?" Dad leaned over and kissed me on top of my head. "In twenty years, she'll be the best district attorney this town's ever seen. I'll be certain to mention this to Officer Whitson. He may need to get over to speak with Angus sooner rather than later." Dad put his hand on Mom's shoulder. "Jenn, do you want to stay here, or are you going home with us? Jackson and I need to change clothes and join the search party."

Grancie answered before Mom could. "Jennifer, you and Julia go with Ben. John and I will follow you out there, and I'll spend the afternoon with you. I want to see the house all decorated anyway, and I'll be there when the men come home."

We left my grandparents' house, and on the drive home Dad called the officer with our idea about too much coincidence. The officer agreed and said a large search party was gathering across the street from the courthouse. As soon as he made assignments, he would pay the Carters a visit to talk to Angus.

Dad reported what Officer Whitson said. Then Dad looked at me in his rearview mirror. "I know this seems like too much of a coincidence, but the more I think of it, there's a good chance these are teenage boys just being teenage boys."

Mom shook her head. "I do hope that's true and they're safe, but if they were just misbehaving, and we were their parents, they might not live to adulthood. Fair warning for you two in the back seat."

Jackson spoke up. "Yeah, Derrick's got this new fancy car. He could just be showing off, like how he can stay out all night. I heard before about the trouble he gets in at school."

Dad answered, "You could be right, and I hope you are. Let this be a lesson to you, son. Part of growing up is stretching your wings, but just make sure how you stretch them doesn't cause a ripple effect that involves so many people being worried about you."

I had been quiet long enough. "Yeah, Jackson, no wing stretching until your frontal lobe is developed, when you're about twenty-five, maybe older for you. Then maybe you won't do something stupid and dangerous."

Dad chuckled. "Yep. You must be careful of those frontal lobes. We needed a laugh, Julia, but we need to hope and pray these boys are safe."

I asked, "Do you think Mr. Lafferty has heard about what's going on?"

We were in the garage. Dad switched the car off and opened his door. "I doubt it. There's no need for him to know, and nobody communicates with him except for us. I can't imagine Mrs. Schumacher would have heard anything."

"But what about Mr. Hornsby? He might have heard something."

"True, but I imagine he's in bed today after getting so banged up last night."

We walked into the house. "Could I call Mr. Lafferty and check on him?"

Dad looked at his watch. "One forty? He could be resting. Maybe we'll call him later this evening. Jackson, dress warmly. It's threatening snow, and the temperature's dropping."

I followed Jackson up the stairs to change clothes. "And don't forget those toasty hand and feet warmers you didn't share with your sister yesterday when we went Christmas tree hunting."

Jackson and Dad were bringing in wood and stacking it on the hearth when G-Pa and Grancie arrived. They put on their jackets. "Okay, ladies, you have wood," Dad said. "Keep that fire going. We don't know when we'll be back, but chances are we'll be cold."

Grancie hugged G-Pa. "We'll keep the fire burning and our prayers marching heavenward. You men stay safe. Do your parts, but stay safe."

Mom added, "And give us a call from time to time. We'll be anxious to hear the news, especially any good news."

I looked at the clock. It was almost five. Mom got up from her chair next to the fire and looked out the window. "It's getting darker out there. Wind's picking up, and snow's coming in tonight. I cannot even imagine what's going through those parents' minds, not knowing where their boys are or if they're safe. And with every passing hour, it grows more likely that something is terribly, terribly wrong."

When the phone rang, she jumped. She didn't say much, but I knew it was Dad. After a few minutes she put the phone down.

"They haven't found them, but Ben said they were the ones to find the car, just no boys. Ben decided to drive around the back roads out near Emerald Crest on a hunch, and that's where they found the car. He said the town's buzzing with all kinds of wild rumors, but things are not looking good."

"Did Dad know if those boys broke Mr. Lafferty's window?"

"Yes. They had plans to. The officer went to the Carters' and interrogated Angus. Apparently, Angus had been getting his information from his older brother, who's friends with Derrick and Wendell. They came clean with what they knew, but Angus's brother has heard nothing from Derrick and Wendell since Friday night."

Grancie moved to the edge of her chair. "This does not sound good to me. And the weather?"

Mom bowed her head and pressed her hands together. "No, it doesn't sound good." She paused. "All this leaves such mystery. What could have happened to those two boys?"

Chapter Thirteen

I WANTED TO CALL H and let him know what was going on, but I knew better. What could he do but worry? Worrying and wondering about something and not being able to do anything about it was like a terrible, itchy rash you couldn't scratch. This was one of those *can'ts* that I wished would become a *can* in a hurry.

Dad brought Jackson and G-Pa home around six o'clock, blowing through the back door like a gust of cold wind. We met them in the kitchen. Dad said, "We're only here for a few minutes for a quick bite, and then we're headed back out."

Mom started pulling things from the refrigerator. "Tonight, in the cold?"

G-Pa answered, "Can't quit looking for those boys. They're most likely out there in the cold going on twenty-four hours now. That's not good."

Grancie asked, "Where's the coffee, Jennifer? I'll make a fresh pot. Julia, see if you can find a thermos. I'll make enough to take with them."

"Good idea. The sheriff's concluded that Derrick and

Wendell are the two who broke the window, and they're still on the Emerald Crest property somewhere, either lost or injured. Either way, we must get to them. He's getting detailed maps of the property, and now it's more like search and rescue."

Mom said, "That's a lot of ground to cover, especially in the dark. But you don't need Jackson, do you? He has school tomorrow."

"Yes, we need him. They're organizing all the athletes from the high school, and we're to meet at the courthouse in twenty minutes. I'm picking up Mr. Hornsby. He and I will try to find where he last saw and heard them last night. That should narrow the search field down a bit. They're getting lights and a couple more ATVs. The more men we have searching, the more ground we can cover."

We stood around the island in the kitchen. Mom asked, "Don't you want to sit down to eat?"

Dad said, "No, we're good. Need to get back to town. I'll eat while I wait on that thermos of coffee."

Mom passed out ham sandwiches and opened a bag of chips. Then Grancie looked at G-Pa. "John, are you going back too?"

"You just heard what Ben said: The more folks we have, the more we can do to find these boys in less time. Time is our enemy right now."

Dad swallowed and wiped the mustard from his mouth. "Speaking of things to do … Jenn, I need you and Mother and Julia to go out to Emerald Crest. Julia, you call Mr. Lafferty now and tell him you three are on the way. Take my computer to communicate with him when you get there."

G-Pa interrupted. "There'll be more activity on that property tonight than he's ever seen before. You can keep him informed of what's going on."

"I'll have my cell, and I can call you, Jenn. Then you can type the message for Mr. Lafferty. That way, he'll know what we know."

I had not said a word, but I was hearing *can'ts* turning into *cans*. "I can help too, Dad. I'll keep him calm. I can show him some more about the computer. He can type messages back. He types on the TTY."

"Good girl. Mr. Lafferty will like it that you are there. Maybe you can play the piano and distract him." Dad gulped his coffee. "Go call him right now and let him know you're coming. Then get out there as soon as you can. I don't want all the traffic and lights to surprise him. You must get there first." Dad slapped Jackson on the back. "Grab a snack for your pocket and a couple of extras. Could be a long night. Let's go." He kissed Mom. "Keep your phone near. The remote for the gate is in the glove compartment. Julia knows what to do."

I was dialing H before they were out of the driveway.

He answered quickly. *HL2.*

This is Julia. Coming to see you. Will explain when we get there. Don't worry.

Now? Is this about the window?

Yes. Will be there in fifteen minutes.

Mrs. Schumacher still here.

Bye. Julia

I ran upstairs and got my yellow pad and came back down to help Mom get Dad's laptop ready to go. Grancie was still busy in the kitchen and called out to Mom in the office. "Maybe we should take some cookies or leftover pie or something. I hate to go out there with just a whole basket of trouble and nothing else. Do you have anything? Or we can stop at the house and get the carrot cake."

"Brownies are under the cake stand. You know where the paper plates and foil are. Take whatever you think."

We had on our jackets and were in the car in five minutes with a plate of brownies and a laptop computer. Mom was always cautious. "Nancie, check the glove compartment for the gate opener. I don't want to leave here unless I know we have it."

Grancie looked around and couldn't find it. I hopped out of the back seat and opened the front door to search myself. "Here it is. Just mash this button when we get to the gate at the bottom of the hill."

"Got it."

Mom drove faster than usual. "It's really cold out there, but no snow yet."

Grancie agreed. "And aren't we glad there's no ice? Close your eyes. Not you, Jennifer; you keep driving. But I need to pray. Lord, you know what a mess this is. You know where those two boys are. And if they're in trouble, and it appears they are, I know you're there with them. Please be with every man and boy on this search team tonight. Guide Ben and Mr. Hornsby to the spot where those boys were last seen. Thank you for the moonlight. And Lord, it would be so helpful if it didn't start snowing too. I ask that you calm Mr. Lafferty and help us to make him feel comfortable, and especially help Julia, Lord. Thank you for listening. Amen."

Grancie prayed like God was right there in the front seat. No fancy words like they used at church for Grancie. I could tell she talked to God regularly like that, like she was giving him directions or telling him just what she wanted.

Mom slowed down. "It's so dark out here. Julia, is this where I turn?"

"Yes, ma'am, but go slow. We're almost to the gate, and then we'll start climbing. The lane is narrow, and it has some hairpin turns."

Mom had a death grip on the steering wheel. "Wow, it's been a long while since I was out here. I had forgotten how treacherous this can be in the dark."

"You're doing fine, Jennifer." When we got to the gate, Grancie mashed the right button and the gate opened. "So how do we close it?"

"You close it the same way once we're through the gate." Then I thought. "But don't close it, Grancie. Dad will need to get through, and I don't know if he has another gate opener. And all those other people that are coming. It'll be all right to leave it open."

Mom said, "Smart girl. Always thinking." Mom drove

slowly. "Keep your eyes open for animals. I don't want to hit a deer, and I know they're out here."

Finally, we pulled up in front of the mansion and parked. I hopped out of the car, ran up the steps, and rang the bell. Lights flashed, and Mrs. Schumacher answered the door. I hugged her hard before she had a chance to speak.

"To what do we owe this pleasure?"

"My mom will explain. Where is Mr. Lafferty?"

"He's in the library waiting for you." Mrs. Schumacher turned to Grancie. "Hello! It's been a while. We have two Mrs. Russells tonight. Welcome."

I turned quickly to Mom. "Let me have the laptop. I'll go set it up." I took it from her hand and practically skidded down the long hall to the library.

H was sitting by the fire. I waved and went straight for the desk in the corner—the one where Dad always worked. I opened the case and turned on the laptop. No signing *Hello* or *How are you* tonight. I had the computer open and plugged in by the time Mrs. Schumacher brought Grancie and Mom into the room. They said the mannerly things you're supposed to say when you come to see somebody, and Mrs. Schumacher interpreted for H. I didn't have time for that tonight. At least not this minute.

"Mom, the laptop's ready. You must type fast. He needs to know what's going on before all the action starts."

Mom sat down, and I motioned for H to come to the desk. My mind was going so fast I couldn't think about signing. I just pointed to what Mom was typing. She told him the whole story. And she was good at it. She sugarcoated better than anybody. She didn't use what she called alarming words, so Mr. Lafferty stayed calm.

The grandfather clock struck seven fifteen. The minute Mrs. Schumacher realized what was happening, she turned on all the outside lights. Bright light flooded the garden and the path to the studio.

By the time the clock struck the half hour, I saw Dad's truck through the window. He parked on the north side of the studio. Right behind him came the sheriff's car. Dad called Mom to make certain we were there and had told Mr. Lafferty what was going on. Then he told Mom that somebody was bringing Mrs. Smithson and Mrs. Brady and to ask Mr. Lafferty's permission for them to stay inside the house during the search.

Mr. Lafferty said yes, and Mrs. Schumacher excused herself to make tea. Grancie had been standing, holding the brownies since we got there. Mrs. Schumacher asked her to come to the kitchen with her.

We saw Dad get out of his truck, and we watched Mr. Hornsby hobble to the ATV and climb on behind Dad. Dad started slowly down the path. The sheriff was right on his tail on another ATV. G-Pa followed in the pickup, and behind him were seven more trucks. The truck cabs and beds were filled with men and boys from the school. In this kind of darkness, those big lights might be seen across the whole county. If Derrick and Wendell were on this property, they had more than a good chance of being found with this many people out looking for them.

Before the clock struck eight, the mothers were there, thanking Mrs. Schumacher and Mr. Lafferty for allowing them to stay. They explained that law officers were at their houses in case the boys showed up, but they wanted to be near their husbands and friends in the last likely place their sons were seen. Mrs. Schumacher left the room after she seated the ladies in front of the fire. Mom got up and tried to comfort them.

I watched Mrs. Smithson and Mrs. Brady and remembered my first visit to Emerald Crest, seeing all these things unlike anything I'd ever seen before. But they didn't seem to notice. They just looked tired and like they cared for nothing except for seeing their sons walk through the door. It was quiet in the room until Grancie and Mrs. Schumacher returned with coffee and brownies for everyone.

When Mrs. Schumacher was there to interpret, Mrs. Smithson apologized to H just in case her son had had anything to do with the broken window. H thanked her for the apology and told her he'd read about her son in the paper, how he was a promising young athlete with hopes for scholarships.

Mrs. Smithson, even in her tiredness, couldn't hide the surprise and the pride in her face. That should tell her something about H, I thought. That he was kind and cared about people. I was hoping and hoping that the more people who got to know him, the more it would help change the way the townspeople thought about him.

The clock struck nine and then ten. Mrs. Schumacher asked H if he wanted to go upstairs. He signed *No*. His mother had taught him good manners, and he wasn't about to leave his guests. I imagined he was worried and curious like the rest of us. I was so glad neither Mom nor H mentioned my playing the piano. It was not a night for "Jingle Bells."

Just after the clock struck ten thirty, Mom's phone rang. She listened and didn't speak, but her face said, "Big news." I couldn't tell if it was good or bad, but it was something important. I would have been popping questions like a popcorn popper, but not Mom. She returned her phone to her pocket and began to speak calmly. "We can be grateful. They have found the boys. They are talking to them right now. That's all good news. But apparently there are some injuries, and they're trying to figure out how to get them to safety."

I asked, "What do you mean to safety?"

Mrs. Schumacher was doing her best to keep up with the interpreting. I watched H's face. It was like stone now. I wondered if he was remembering his own injuries when the car hit him and his mother.

Mom continued reporting what Dad had said. "Apparently the other night when they were running away, they ran quite a ways down the road that cuts through the property. But then they left the road and ran out through a heavily forested area, and they fell into a deep ravine that's more like the opening to a cave. They couldn't climb or crawl out."

Mrs. Brady looked at Mrs. Smithson. "We must go to them. Somebody tell us how to get there."

Mom said, "They're already sending someone for you now. You're to meet the driver outside next to the studio. Ben said a paramedic and another guy rappelled down to the boys. They're assessing the injuries now, but the boys may have to be airlifted out. They can't climb, and it's too steep to carry them out. They have requested helicopter assistance, so they're just waiting now."

Mrs. Brady and Mrs. Smithson began to cry. They held each other like holding on would keep their boys safe. Mrs. Schumacher led them out the garden room door and across the brick path through the garden to the studio. We watched as a truck drove up and in seconds they were gone. If Jackson Russell ever did anything stupid like that and caused Mom and Dad and all these people this kind of pain, I would set his hair on fire and pull his fingernails and toenails out one by one.

Just as the clock struck eleven fifteen, we heard the helicopter. H couldn't hear it, so I pointed to the window and up. We could see flashing lights in the sky, and I fingerspelled *h-e-l-i-c-o-p-t-e-r.*

H smiled and fingerspelled *N-o-w w-e p-r-a-y f-o-r s-a-f-e-t-y.*

Yes.

There was not a mean bone in H's body. Those boys had done him harm. They had upset his life and caused lots of people to be worried, and I was angry at them. I didn't want them to be hurt or anything like that, but I was mad and so tired and sleepy. I curled up like a cat on the rug in front of the fireplace. H rolled over near me and signed *Sweet sleep, Julia.*

Just after midnight, the doorbell rang. I jumped up from where I was and ran to the door with Mrs. Schumacher. It was the

Russell men. They looked tired and cold. They entered the library and went straight to the fire, shedding their coats and gloves.

Mom got up and hugged Dad and Jackson, and Grancie kissed G-Pa like she hadn't seen him in a month of Sundays.

Dad started by apologizing to Mr. Lafferty for all the activity and for invading his home and privacy and for keeping him up so late.

Mrs. Schumacher voiced for Mr. Lafferty. "No need to apologize. Tell us about the boys. Are they safe?"

Dad told the story of how they'd found Derrick and Wendell after more than an hour. "They're both dehydrated and probably have hypothermia and are certainly in shock. One of Derrick's knees is busted up pretty bad and he's got a compound fracture below the knee in the other leg. Too early to tell how much blood he lost. Wendell fared a bit better with a nasty bump on his head, probably a concussion, and a few other bruises and contusions. Could have a dislocated shoulder. But it seems that Derrick might have cushioned Wendell's fall."

I was totally awake now. "But, Dad, where did they find them?"

"This area is known for having caves. Seems like these boys found one when they weren't looking. They just ran right through the forest until there was no more ground and went down the rabbit hole, so to speak."

"So they heard you and they called out?"

"Yes. They heard us. Otherwise, they might have never been found. I think Wendell might have been unconscious for a short while, and I doubt Derrick was able to move very much. Apparently, after he came to, Wendell applied some kind of crude tourniquet to Derrick's leg. That helped with the bleeding."

"But they'll be all right, won't they?"

G-Pa answered, "They're airlifting them to the hospital in Elkins. We'll know more in twenty-four hours, but with the good Lord's help, they'll live. I imagine Derrick is looking at some surgery and months of rehab."

I was still curious. "Did anybody ask them why they were out here breaking windows?"

Dad looked straight at me. "Julia, this was not the time to ask the boys that question. I can tell you they were both traumatized."

Then G-Pa added, "We found out from Angus's older brother that some of the high school boys have a club. He assured us it wasn't a gang or drug related, just a club. And there were things they had to do to get to be a member, sort of like initiation. Seems they had to prove their bravery."

I knew what G-Pa wasn't saying. Like Angus said, those boys called this a creepy house and told wild stories about ghosts and buried treasure. But G-Pa wasn't about to say anything like that in front of Mr. Lafferty.

Dad started to put on his jacket and turned to H. "I'll get someone out here tomorrow to get started on the repairs. Again, I'm so sorry, but I don't think we'll have any more broken windows. There will be some activity out here the next couple of days, then things should settle down. You'll need to decide what you want to do about Mr. Hornsby now that the threat is over."

Mrs. Schumacher spoke for H. "We'd like him to stay. We need someone on the property taking care of things. We don't need another near-tragedy at Emerald Crest."

"I agree, and Edgar needs the job. He's good and faithful, and he'll do you well. I'll give him a call first thing in the morning. I think we can change his work schedule to days though. He'll be so grateful to know he still has a job, especially this close to Christmas. We'll be leaving now, but thank you for taking care of my family tonight." He shook H's hand.

H signed, and Mrs. Schumacher voiced, "You have a beautiful family, one that's well taken care of, Ben. And these other families will have medical bills, especially the boy with the leg injury. If they need any help, I want to be the one to help."

H had let his secret out. He trusted our whole family.

We said our goodnights, and Mrs. Schumacher closed the door behind our tribe. Grancie made it to the bottom step before she stopped. "Would you look at that—those large flakes? It's just beginning to snow. Thank you, God, for holding it back till now."

Dad and G-Pa said, "Amen."

Jackson rode with Mom and Grancie in the car, and I sat between Dad and G-Pa in the truck. They were tired and quiet, but I couldn't hold it any longer. "Who does that? Who offers to pay the medical bills of the boys who trashed his house and caused so much trouble?"

Dad answered softly, "A man whose heart pumps goodness."

I would have to think about that, but not tonight.

Chapter Fourteen

MONDAY MORNING CAME ESPECIALLY EARLY. There hadn't been this much excitement in Sycamore Hill since the fire at the courthouse. I was hoping school might be called off because of the snow and most of the town being out so late, but Mom woke me early. I had to face Angus today, but I had an answer if he got mean. Mom always said you catch more flies with honey. Now, I never figured why anybody would want to catch flies anyway, but I knew if Angus was mean to me, and then I got mean, he'd just get meaner. So I was ready for him.

I dressed in a hurry and went downstairs. I was mostly curious about all the phone calls and what else was going on this early.

When the phone rang during breakfast, Dad disappeared to his office. On the way to school, I asked him why all the calls this morning. All he said was, "Just the fallout from the broken windows and the rescue last night. Nothing you need to know, and nothing you can say anything about if you did know, so it's best if you don't know."

"Yes, sir, I got it. But I still want to know." The look I got from the rearview mirror kept me quiet.

Dad dropped Jackson off at school first. When we got to my school and Dad got out to open my door, he said, "Julia, don't you get into it with Angus today. If he causes problems, you just stay quiet. He can't argue with silence. And if he won't let it go, you tell Mrs. Grayson and let her handle it. Do you understand?"

"Yes, sir. I won't have anything to do with trouble today." I wasn't about to tell Dad I had a plan. I wasn't waiting on Angus to say something to me, and he'd just better not mention snitching. I planned to pour honey on that idea before he had a chance to open his mouth.

He wasn't in the classroom when I got there. Snow had caused delays this morning, but he got there before the bell rang.

I walked right up to him. "How does it feel to be a hero this morning, Angus?"

He looked at me like I might have been speaking in another language.

"Just think, what you were able to tell the police officer saved Derrick and Wendell. They could have both died right there in that cave, and nobody would have ever known what happened to them."

Angus stood up a little straighter. His face looked like he wanted to smile, but he didn't. "Yeah, I'm glad they're okay. My brother helped too. He even went out to look for them."

"You and your brother are brave. It takes a lot of courage to do what you did, to do the right thing and speak to the police. The whole town will be thanking you."

The bell rang, and Mrs. Grayson rescued me when she told us all to take our seats. No more time for talking to Angus. It hadn't been so bad after all.

Dad took me out to Emerald Crest on Tuesday afternoon. H was at the table in the library just like always, and we started to work carving detail on the feathers. He laid the pheasant feathers I gave him on the table in front of us. Mrs. Schumacher had a quiet conversation with Dad in the corner while H and I worked, then she left the room.

I could tell H had something on his mind. He carved and brushed away the shavings, but he kept looking over his shoulder at Dad. Then he moved away from the table and went to the doorway of the library. He pressed a button on the wall under the light switch, and a bell rang. Mrs. Schumacher appeared in no time. They signed something to each other. Then she announced, "I'll be bringing tea and cookies in just a few moments." Then she looked at me. "And Julia, afterwards Mr. Lafferty wants you to see his studio."

We had tea, and then I was on my way to see H's studio—a real studio where he'd worked and created for years. Mom had a studio out back of our house, but it was just a dressed-up barn with some windows where she could paint without worrying about a mess. But our house could never be a mess.

Mrs. Schumacher had collected our teacups and put them on the tray with the teapot and cookies. "Julia," she said, "would you like to come with me? Mr. Lafferty wants me to take you to see where he usually works when the weather is much warmer. We'll stop in the kitchen first." I had thought H would take me and explain everything I saw, but he didn't. I figured it out. This was his way of getting rid of me so he could talk to Dad.

"Yes, ma'am. And I'd like to see your kitchen too. I help my Mom and Grancie in the kitchen sometimes. They talk a lot about kitchens. They're good cooks, like you, Mrs. Schumacher. Oh, and Grancie said she'd be happy to give you her pound-cake cookie recipe." Actually, I wanted to see that whole house, every room, and what was behind every door, but the studio was a good place to start.

"Why, thank you, Julia. I'm a much better baker than a

cook, and I do look forward to getting that recipe from your grandmother. I so enjoyed my visit with her the other night. Even under such dire circumstances, it was good to have guests."

I followed her down a hallway beside the garden room. There was the window all boarded up. "They didn't fix the window yet?"

"No, not yet. That was one of the largest windows in the house, and they must order it special. I'm afraid we'll be looking at the board for another couple of weeks. It keeps the wind and the cold out, but I do miss the view of the garden. From right here in the kitchen, I can see Mr. Lafferty when he's in the garden and the lights from the studio."

That kitchen was as big as a house. Grancie would have thought she had died and gone to kitchen heaven in there. White cabinets with glass doors everywhere. I could have taken a bath in the sink. And there must have been an acre of green marble countertops. Mrs. Schumacher set the tray down on an island bigger than our kitchen. She patted the marble. "This is the best. It's marble, and it's where I roll out all my pastries and cookies."

"You could make enough cookies for the whole town in here." Then I got an idea. "I'm so glad you agreed to the Christmas party, and it will be so much fun. Grancie and Mom will be making cookies for the next three weeks."

"Oh, yes, I had a few words with your grandmother when she was here Saturday evening. I told her I would enjoy making cookies for the party as well."

I walked around the island and ran my hand across the top. "I'll bet that made Grancie happy, and what would make her even happier is if you invited her and Mom out here to bake cookies in this kitchen. You could make this whole house smell like Christmas."

"Having them come out would double my pleasure in baking." She unfolded a tea towel and draped it over the cookies and teapot.

"You should ask them. I know they'd come."

"Oh, I must ask Mr. Lafferty first. It is his house, remember."

"But don't you live here too?"

"I did for a few years, and then I bought my own home. I'm thinking of moving back. It would be better for me and for Mr. Lafferty if I were here. But it would still be his home." She paused. "I'll make it all right with him to invite your mom and grandmother, and we'll keep the secret. He'll never know we're baking cookies for a Christmas party at Emerald Crest. Come along, I must show you the studio."

There was still snow in the garden. I could see the lights were on in the studio. It had a whole wall of windows facing the garden. Mr. Hornsby was in there working. Mrs. Schumacher opened the door and announced we were entering. He stood up and invited us in. "I'm working on these cabinets, doing some repairs and cleaning. By springtime, Mr. Lafferty will think he has a new studio. What do you think, Helena?"

"Why, I think Mr. Lafferty will be so grateful and so surprised. You do such beautiful work, Edgar. He will appreciate your craftsmanship. There are a few other projects in the house that could use your expertise too. And winter might be the best time to do them."

I was glad to know at least Mrs. Schumacher and Mr. Hornsby were on a first-name basis now. That meant they were getting along.

She showed me around the studio. Unfinished birds, blocks of wood, and stacks of boards lined the shelves and walls. The worktable fit right under the windows, and I pictured H sitting there working, having the best-ever view of the whole garden.

Perched in the window sat a pair of cardinals on a limb. They were painted just like the ones he'd given Dad for Christmas. And above them was a bright red one hanging from the ceiling with fishing line. It looked like my baby cousin Jake's mobile over his crib, only that redbird was some kind of pretty with her wings spread, making flying look more fun than anything.

Mr. Hornsby must have seen me looking at them. "Ain't they something? Just finished polishing 'em with some good oil. Got years of dust off 'em."

"Mr. Lafferty will like that. He really likes cardinals." Mr. Hornsby probably didn't know yet why H liked cardinals, and I couldn't tell him.

Mrs. Schumacher stood behind me. I turned and asked her, "Could we go back inside?"

"Certainly, child, you must be cold." She took my hand, and we walked back through the garden.

"Thank you for showing me the studio, and I shouldn't ask, but could you show me the big living room where we will have the party? It would help me if I could see it. My dad can help me draw up a plan so that when this party rolls in here, everyone will know where to go and how to get ready. We'll have to do it in a hurry."

"Good idea. Come along. I'll show you." She led me down the hall past the library. Dad and H were still huddled in the corner, H looking over Dad's shoulder at the computer screen. They were talking business, and that's why he'd sent me away.

Mrs. Schumacher opened large wooden double doors to the biggest room I had ever seen. It was like a ballroom in a princess movie. Another acre of green marble on the floors and glass walls on three sides. The furniture sat covered in sheets. My eyes went straight to the piano at the end of the room. It was covered in sheets too, but I knew it was the piano. Dad had been right; it was bigger than the one in the garden room.

Mrs. Schumacher almost twirled around, pointing every-thing out to me. "Oh, this room was the loveliest, and I'll make certain it is lovely again for this party. No sheets, only polished furniture and inviting chairs."

"This is perfect. I can see it now." I pointed to the end of the room where the piano was. "There's where we'll do the play, and then the choir will stand next to the piano to sing. Oh, and Piper has this whole room for her dance. She's my best friend, and Mrs. Schumacher, she is the most beautiful dancer you will ever see."

"And you're the most beautiful pianist."

I felt my cheeks turning red. "Oh, no. This room deserves the best-ever pianist, and I'm not it."

"But you will play, won't you? Mr. Lafferty will be so disappointed if you don't."

"Yes, ma'am." Butterflies filled my chest again just looking at this room. It was perfect. Mom and Grancie would be baking with Mrs. Schumacher, and this party was going to be better than I had planned. It might be the beginning of something that I didn't know about yet.

Finally, Wednesday came, and our first rehearsal getting ready for the surprise party. Mrs. Wilson, Piper, and her mom had been to our house last night to work on the play. They liked my story. It was a simple one, but Mrs. Wilson said it had lots of meanings.

Piper and her mom decided on all the movements and motions and made their notes. Mom told them all about the costumes the sewing ladies were making and that Dad was providing the prop.

Mrs. Wilson assigned the parts. It wasn't really that hard with only three boys and nine girls and nobody speaking. She thought I should read the story since I wrote it, but I didn't want to do that, so I asked her to be the reader. She agreed on the condition that I would read my story at choir rehearsal. I promised to get Mrs. Walker a copy so she could be ready to sign for H.

Our choir met in a small room down the hall from the

sanctuary. Mrs. Wilson had named our choir Melody Makers, and then she'd gone candy crazy with M&M's for our nickname. She found a poster of nothing but M&M's to put on the door. Then she always had a bowl of M&M's with peanuts on the piano. They were treats for good behavior.

Most of the time Mrs. Wilson acted like she had eaten too many M&M's, and tonight was one of those nights. She used her excited voice to tell the Melody Makers and the other two adult workers about the big surprise Christmas party. "Why, this surprise party is going to be such a surprise for everyone! You won't even know where it is until the day of the party. It's hush-hush, but it's going to be so wonderful, and something you'll remember." Then she looked at me. "Julia, would you come up here, please?"

I knew what she wanted, so I brought my folder with my story. I had to stand there while she explained what mime was and that nobody had to learn lines. "And after Julia reads her story to you, Piper and her mom will help us stage it. We will only have one prop, so we'll just have to imagine that when we're rehearsing this week." Finally, she tapped me on the shoulder. "Julia, please read us your amazing story."

It really wasn't my amazing story. It was the oldest and best story ever. I'd just written it Julia-style. I held up my folder and began to read.

Once upon forever, in a land nearer than you can imagine, there lived a king and all his people. He was called King of the High Mountain. It was beautiful and peaceful on the High Mountain where he lived. The forest was greener than any other forest down below. The flowers were more colorful than any other flowers anywhere. And the music was more beautiful than any music ever heard. The sun shone on the High Mountain all the time. There were no storms, only a mist that watered the mountain and made rainbows.

The king lived in a castle—the most beautiful castle ever. And there were houses, beautiful houses, on the High Mountain. But the houses were all empty, and the King was so lonely. If he only had neighbors …

The King of the High Mountain looked at all his people in the valley below. The men and women worked hard in the fields to grow food, but storms and pests destroyed their crops. Many of them went hungry. They built shelters to live in, but the winds came and blew them down. The sun stopped shining every day, and the darkness caused the people to get lost and hurt. Some of the people got sick, and some of them were mean to each other.

The King of the High Mountain called down to his people and invited them to live on the mountaintop where everything was beautiful, but they could not find the path to get to the top. The King sent messages with maps and instructions, but the people ignored them and did not pay attention. They just kept on doing things their way, the hard way, down in the valley.

One day the King said to himself, The people cannot get here by themselves. I must send someone to show them the path. They will follow him all the way to the top of the High Mountain. The King thought and thought about who should go down the mountain. If I send a messenger, the people might not listen and follow him. But if I send my son with my invitation, they will follow him all the way up to the High Mountain. So that's what the King did.

The Prince traveled a long road down from the High Mountain. He went into the valleys to all the men, and he went to all the women and even the children. He handed each of them a beautiful invitation from his father, the King of the High Mountain. And one by one, they followed him, and he led them all the way to the top of the High Mountain.

The King was so happy to have neighbors, and the people were so happy to be there. They could not believe how beautiful everything was on the High Mountain, and they never thought of living in the valley below again. They roamed the green forests and swam in *clear streams and ate the best food ever every day. And there was no darkness to frighten them or cause them to lose their way. They lived peacefully on the High Mountain.*

This is the story of Christmas. This is the real story of living happily ever after.

I took my seat, and Mrs. Wilson clapped like she'd never heard a story before or was giving me a standing ovation or something. I even thought I saw a tear in her eye. "Oh, Julia, this is the best story ever. I can see all of you beautiful children now bringing this story to life." She paused and wiped her eye. "This is going to be the best surprise Christmas party ever. Now, Piper, will you and your mom come up? And let's get to work, Melody Makers."

We got home after church Wednesday night. I put my backpack on the breakfast table. Mom went for the teakettle, and Jackson went straight for the refrigerator. His head was usually either there or on his pillow or the arm of the sofa. He put the gallon of milk on the island and started looking for a snack.

Dad followed us in and loosened his tie. He spoke like he was making an announcement. "You will be happy to know that everything is working out."

He had my attention. "Is there something that wasn't working out?"

"Good question, Julia. And yes, there was. Come to find out, there were four more boys involved with the other two broken windows out at Emerald Crest. When I called the police the other night about the third broken window, that meant that the police would have to file charges against the boys. Mr. Lafferty was mighty upset about that. He did not want them charged. He felt they and their families had suffered enough already."

Jackson was on his second glass of milk, and I kept my eye

on him inhaling the cookies. "Jackson, could you save me just one swallow of milk and one cookie?"

He rolled his eyes and kept chewing.

When Jackson went to the pantry for the peanut butter, I grabbed two cookies and made a face at Dad. "So why don't you just drop the charges?"

"Can't. You can't just drop charges when a case has been filed. Listen up, Julia. Justice System 101. The complaint had already been sent to the district attorney, and he had already filed it with the court."

"So, Dad, how do you plan to turn this *can't* into a *can* and make Mr. Lafferty happy?"

"The only way to make a *can* out of this situation was to persuade the DA to dismiss the case. DAs don't usually dismiss a case if they have evidence and can prove their case, and he has the evidence and *could* prove it. That meant my only chance was to let him know that Mr. Lafferty would be a reluctant witness. It took a bit of convincing, but the DA thought better of it and dropped the case. I persuaded him that the parents of these boys would make amends with Mr. Lafferty and they'd also make certain these boys were disciplined for their actions."

"Yeah for Dad! You turned that *can't* into a *can*, and you made Mr. Lafferty happy and all those boys and their parents."

"I saved myself some time, and I saved the taxpayers some money. And in case you're wondering, there's no more club on campus that requires boys to do stupid, destructive things in the name of bravery. You get that, Jackson?"

"Yes, sir. Do you know how Derrick and Wendell are?"

"I heard today Wendell's back home. It'll be a while before Derrick sees the outside of a hospital. Two more surgeries to go on his leg."

I drank a glass of milk and headed upstairs, where I showered, dressed for bed, and sat at my desk watching my sign-language DVD. I searched to learn the signs for *go, tell, mountain, over, hills, everywhere, Jesus, born*. I practiced them

187

over and over. "Go, Tell It on the Mountain" was H's favorite song, and it had to be perfect.

I crawled into bed and began to think of that room, and I remembered another song. If Piper could dance her way across that room and she didn't even know Mr. Lafferty, and if the whole choir could sing, and they didn't know him, then I would sing him a song all by myself in his language. *I can, and I will.*

I pulled out the brown bag from under the bed and finished the rest of a granny square. Eight minutes and lights were out. I think I hummed the song softly until I fell asleep.

Chapter Fifteen

MOM OPENED THE LID TO the box on the counter. "The sewing ladies at church finished the costumes. Grancie picked them up at church yesterday and brought them out this afternoon. Want to see?"

"Oh, yes. Did she bring the crown?" I remembered she'd said the crown would really be something.

"Well, let's see." Mom folded back the lid. "Here it is, right on top." She lifted it carefully out of the box and set it down.

I ran my hand over the metal and the jewels. "Wow, Grancie was right. This is no cardboard crown with glitter. Let's see the costumes." *Robby will look like a real prince with this crown.*

"Mr. Hornsby helped us with the crown. He was there when Grancie and I were out at Emerald Crest baking cookies with Mrs. Schumacher. He heard us talking about making the costumes and that we were having some trouble coming up with a crown that wasn't cardboard. He volunteered, said there was copper sheeting in the studio that would work. And when we left, we had the beginnings of a crown."

"Looks like Grancie got busy with her glue gun and velvet and these fake emeralds and rubies."

"Yes, and I think she had a lot of fun."

"I know. She likes making things. You know, Mom, I like Mr. Hornsby. Dad says he's a good man. And I like it that Mr. Lafferty is not out there all alone and he has somebody besides Mrs. Schumacher looking out for him."

"Your dad's right, and I think Mr. Hornsby will be with Mr. Lafferty a very long time. He works hard, and he'll take care of that property and Mr. Lafferty. And the good news is that Mrs. Schumacher is selling her house to him in a way that he can afford it. It will be his family's very first home. And she's moving into Emerald Crest this week."

"Does that mean that the Hornsbys will be in their new house before Christmas?"

"I think so. Your dad's handling the paperwork to make it happen. Mrs. Schumacher is leaving most everything that's in the house. She doesn't need it, and the Hornsbys don't have very much."

"This should be a great Christmas for his family." I tried to move the box lid so I could see more.

"For certain it will be a good Christmas for them." Mom lifted the folded costumes out of the box. "Look, no striped bathrobes or old towels. These are real costumes. And look what the sewing ladies made for the girls to wear. Each one has a shawl and a sash to match. And they're all different."

I couldn't see over the box lid. "What about the costume for the Prince? Do you see it? It's supposed to be purple."

"Do you mean this one?" Mom pulled out a purple toga with a lighter purple sash trimmed in gold ribbon.

"That has to be it. Robby will look nice in that."

"Robby?" Mom glared at me. "Look nice?"

"Robby's the Prince, Mom. He's supposed to look nice."

Mom raised her eyebrows. "Oh, we certainly want Robby the Prince to look nice." She folded the costume and put it back in the box. "How's your song coming?"

"Fine, I think. Mrs. Wilson will play for me, and I can sing it. But it's not easy signing and singing." Even just talking about it, my hands started moving. I had been practicing so much I could hardly keep my hands still anymore.

"Don't you just sign the words? That should come easy for you."

"Oh, no. It's not like that, Mom. It's not real American Sign Language just to sign every word I sing. That would be like signing English, and that's not American Sign Language. Mrs. Walker said I had to understand the song and think about what it meant, and I had to sign the concepts."

"I get it. That's way more difficult."

I waved my arms in the air over my head. "Really way more difficult." Then I stood still. "It's like communicating in three languages. I'm singing English words and signing American Sign Language, and then there's the whole music thing. That's like a language too."

Mom curled a ringlet of my hair around her finger. "Glad it's you, kid, and not me. But I have faith. You can do it."

"I think I could do it in my sleep."

Mom picked up the box to move it to the laundry room. "Maybe Robby, the look-nice-Prince, will think you're pretty special singing and signing."

I turned so Mom couldn't see me. My face was getting hot, and that Russell streak down my forehead had to be turning red. "Maybe not."

"Oh, Julia, I know it will be a beautiful moment, and Mr. Lafferty will be so moved and so appreciative. And then there's the whole play thing that you wrote just for him."

I remembered the set, and the subject needed changing. "I almost forgot. Did Dad and G-Pa finish the mountain?"

Mom was back in the kitchen by then. "G-Pa was supposed to pick it up today. He and your dad cut it out of plywood, and G-Pa got one of his retired friends who is an artist to paint it. But G-Pa thought the King of the High Mountain might need a stool to stand on, so they built a ladder-like stool for the back of the mountain."

"I hope they can get it through the front door."

"Not to worry. It's not that big. But you did name it the High Mountain, and they wanted the playwright to be happy."

"Can we use it Wednesday for our last rehearsal?"

"Grancie told G-Pa to take it to the church and leave it in the M&M room."

"Fantastic. It's all coming together, Mom."

Jackson built a fire after supper and turned on television. I didn't think that boy ever studied anything but a game. Mom joined me at the table by the window. "Are you sure this is what you want to do?"

I had the scissors, pen, glitter glue, the hole puncher, white paper, and gold ribbon all out in front of me. "Yes, ma'am. It's important. Grancie gave me the idea."

"And how many do we need to make?"

"Well, at first it was only going to be eleven for the kids singing. But now I think it needs to be for everybody there. Grancie said that would be a special touch and everyone would have a remembrance of this evening to take home with them."

Dad came in from his office and walked over to the table. "What are you making?"

I handed him the script to the play. "There's a part in the play when the King of the High Mountain's son gives everyone a beautiful invitation. We're making the invitation. And then the Prince will hand out something special for everyone in the room. Grancie said this was going to be a special moment, and everybody needed a keepsake to help them to remember it."

"Your grancie's like that. She's memorialized things as long as I can remember. My first report card, the cat having kittens, family trips—if we did it, Grancie made it special. Most folks do that kind of thing with photos, but she does it with her pen and paper and poetry."

Dad read Grancie's poem and then through my script. "This is good, Julia. Now I know why you needed a mountain. So how many of these keepsakes are you making?"

"I think about sixty will do." I started counting sheets of paper.

"Sixty? I thought you said about twenty-five when you started this."

"But we have more. Mrs. Wilson sent out a letter about the surprise party, and now all the parents want to come and bring their other children. Then there's Mrs. Schumacher, and I'm inviting Mr. Hornsby and his family."

"You sure you have enough glitter glue?" Dad chuckled.

"Maybe not. But we're writing the messages and punching holes for the ribbon tonight."

Dad tapped his finger on the table. Mom was a hand-wringer, but Dad tapped when he was thinking. "Jackson, turn off that television and turn on the Christmas music to loud, and get yourself over here. We have a family project, and Mom and Julia need our help."

Jackson didn't like it much to begin with, but we had a good time around the table. Dad divided it up so that each of us made fifteen invitations. "Let's at least get all these written first, and then you can decorate them, Julia. I don't think Jackson and I would be very good at that. But now, hole-punching? Jackson, that'll give your muscles a good workout. Just think—sixty repetitions."

I wrote the first message and passed it to Jackson. He copied it and passed it on to Dad and then to Mom. Before long, we were into writing. Mom, being her cautious self, said, "You should read every word when you finish. This is an important message, and there should be no mistakes. And in your best printing, Jackson."

"Yes, these are Grancie's words. Best get them right."

While we wrote, we listened to "O Little Town of Bethlehem" and "Away in a Manger" and all the carols that Dad liked. Sometimes we talked, and sometimes we sang along, but we all copied Grancie's words.

MEMORIES OF HOLY NIGHTS

Silent days, but a holy night—that moment in
time when the world was made right,
When God came near in the mire and manger,
Breath of heaven, to the world a stranger, yet hope for us all.
Stars blazed, angels praised, a mother gazed into the face of God.
'Twas a moment in time when life was reborn.
'Twas a holy night.
Silent days, but a holy night—a moment in
time when the world seemed right,
When the King of the High Mountain
came near in the music and mime,
Child messengers for such a time, as joy-bringers to us all.
Bells rang, children sang, hearts were changed
with the return of Christmas.
'Twas a moment in time when memories were reborn.
'Twas a holy night.

After a little while, Mom got up and came back with a basket of popcorn and cups of hot apple cider. In less than a couple of hours, we were done. Invitations all written, all punched, and all with one gold ribbon tied in the corner. I looked at that stack of folded cards, and I looked at that three-inch tube of glitter glue. Dad was right. I didn't have enough, but maybe Grancie's poem didn't really need glitter. Maybe it was just right as it was.

Dad stood up and cracked his knuckles. "Well, this evening didn't turn out the way I planned. It turned out better. Jackson, turn off the music and turn on the game. Maybe we can catch the last quarter."

Mom helped me clear and clean the table. I put all the cards in a box, taped it shut, and took it to the laundry room with the box of costumes. "Thanks, everybody. I'm going upstairs."

Mom asked, "To bed or to practice?"

I needed to finish one more round of crocheting to put the second lap quilt together. *Jesus, forgive me for this fib, but it's for another good reason.* "I might practice signing for a little while, then I'll be under those warm covers and out with the lights." I hugged Mom, kissed her cheek, and thanked her for helping. I hugged Dad too and waved goodnight to Jackson. "No need to come up. I've had my goodnight hugs."

Grancie was right about a lot of things, and she was right about crocheting being a good time to think, especially when I was crocheting the edging and didn't have to count. I had plenty to think about. A lot of things had started when I met Mr. Lafferty. He became my friend, and he was teaching me sign language and bird carving, and he took me with him to sit under the chestnut oaks to feed the birds. *He will be so surprised when we all show up to bring him a party.*

Single crochet, slip stitch, single crochet, slip stitch. I thought about the party and the beautiful room and all the people. It was going to be something—much more than I first imagined. And so many people had gotten involved to help. Mom and Dad, Mrs. Wilson, Piper and her mom, Grancie and G-Pa, and Mrs. Schumacher and Mr. Hornsby. And then there were the ladies who'd made the costumes and G-Pa's friend who painted the mountain. And tonight even Jackson had helped. Lots of people had worked on this party, and most of them didn't even know why. But when it was all over and they found out, they would be glad for what they'd done to help.

But not all the things that had happened were good. There were the broken windows and the boys getting into trouble and Derrick getting hurt bad. But even with that, Mr. Hornsby had gotten a good job and a new house, and Mrs. Schumacher was able to move back to Emerald Crest.

Grancie was so right about moments that change everything, like the moment I'd met Mr. Lafferty and the moment Derrick fell into the cave and got hurt. Those moments had changed things for lots of people. Derrick didn't know when he picked up one rock that it would change his life and affect his whole family. And when those boys decided to break windows to prove themselves, they didn't know it would change Mr. Hornsby's life too. Now Mr. Hornsby had a good job and a house, and neither Mrs. Schumacher nor Mr. Lafferty would be living alone ever again.

I was glad something good had come out of what those boys did even though they didn't know it. There was a lot I didn't know too, but I hoped something good would come out of this surprise Christmas party.

As soon as I walked into the library, I saw Mr. Lafferty, but no wood-carving tools or feathers were on the table. Today he had on a heavy jacket, his plaid tam, and a blanket over his legs and one around his shoulders. He turned his laptop around to show me what he'd typed. *Not a day for carving. The white-crowned sparrows are back. Come quietly with me.* Then H put on his gloves and rolled out of the room and down the hall to the garden room.

He didn't stop until he came to a pile of brush near the end of the brick path. The brush looked like someone had put it there on purpose, and there was a small stool nearby. He pointed at the stool and then at me. I sat down on the stool, and he stopped right next to me. He reached beside him in his chair and pulled out a can. He poured birdseed onto the ground and the brick path and then into his gloved hand. He nodded to me.

I held my hand out for the seed. There was no need for him to instruct. I just watched him and did what he did. I was glad the wind wasn't blowing and there was no snow on the ground. From where we sat, I could see the glass windows in the garden room, and the lamp in the library window where Dad sat at the desk in the corner with his computer. Mrs. Schumacher was to my left in the kitchen, rolling something out on the marble-topped island.

It didn't seem long before I heard a whir in the brush beside us. I didn't move. Neither did H. Three medium-sized birds alighted on the brush. They had brownish wings and gray bellies, and they beat their wings and then settled down. When they were still, I saw the white crown, almost like a tuft of white hair with black lines outlining it. I knew this was the bird H was looking for—the white-crowned sparrow.

It was not a long wait before they hopped from the brush onto the ground and began eating the seeds H had put there. They didn't stay long and flew away. The excitement of their arrival was over. But even when they flew, H didn't move a muscle.

Neither did I. I moved nothing but my eyes in the quiet, and I saw the windows in the great living room at the other end of the house. In the silence, I closed my eyes and daydreamed about the light and the joy that would fill that room on Sunday afternoon. I was imagining when I heard it—the birdsong sounded like *birdie, birdie, birdie.* And then there was silence. I waited and didn't even want to breathe. There it was again, but different, more like *cheer, cheer, cheer.*

H looked at me, pointed upward at birds flying over, smiled big, and brushed his hands together to get rid of the birdseed. Then he pulled out another can. I did exactly what he did and held out my hand. He poured kernels of sunflower seeds in my hand and then into his and put the can away.

Then he again sat like a statue. I couldn't really see his face because he was beside me, but I felt his stillness and his excitement. I slowly turned my head and froze. We waited. The *birdie, birdie, birdie* sound was behind us now. Then I felt the whir. The reddest cardinal I'd ever seen flew right over my shoulder and landed in H's hand. The male cardinal picked up a seed. I could hear it when he cracked it with his beak. Then another whir over my shoulder. But this time, the female alighted in my hand and picked up a seed. She was so light that I wouldn't have known she was there if I weren't looking or hadn't felt the breeze her wings created. I didn't think I could stay still.

And then the male hopped over to my hand, picked up a seed, and fed it to his mate. He was so red with his black mask and red crest, and she was brown with a crest and a deep-orange beak. Her wings looked like they had been dusted with Mom's blush. Nobody but H would believe a pair of cardinals was feeding from my hand. They weren't there long, but long enough that I knew this would be the first of many afternoons in H's garden. I had been there before and even out to where his parents and mother were buried under the chestnut oaks two weeks ago when the cedar waxwings were moving through. I had been still and quiet just like H and watched them feed from his hands but not mine. Today was different—it was the day H passed his gift to me.

After the birds flew, we both froze like statues. I wanted them to come back, but the sun was way below the mountain behind us, and the sky was getting dark. H clapped his hands together. I was so happy I jumped up, threw the sunflower seeds to the wind, and hugged H's neck. I was so happy I might have even hugged Jackson's neck if he'd been there to see me. When I let go of H, he just smiled and clapped his hands again, like he was happy for me and proud that he had succeeded. He didn't hug back, but that was okay. I knew he would someday.

I wondered how H had known the cardinals were there. He couldn't hear their chirping. I signed my question and he answered with more signs and gestures. I was amazed that he'd seen their shadows and recognized their flight pattern. H knew everything about birds.

I'd been coming to H's house every Tuesday afternoon now for months. He had taught me so many signs. I had carved two feathers and was working on a bird. I had learned to sharpen my carving tools. And now he'd taught me how to be so still and quiet that a bird would feed from my hand.

Chapter Sixteen

O N WEDNESDAY AFTERNOON, I COULD hardly wait to walk through the door at church—that door with the M&M poster on it. I wanted to see the mountain Dad and G-Pa had built. I wanted to see my choir friends dressed in their costumes, and especially Piper. She'd made up her own ballet dance as a Christmas angel. She would look like an angel for sure. Mrs. Walker planned to be there to see it all today and to hear Mrs. Wilson read the story. I was so ready for this—our dress rehearsal. Mrs. Wilson always told us that nothing would happen in performance that had not already happened many times in rehearsal. I hoped she was right.

Mom and Grancie were there to help with costumes, and we used fake cards for the Prince to hand out. I handed them to Robby and explained. He looked like a prince in purple.

Grancie had made the emerald-green costume for me. Maybe she thought it would look good with my hair and blue eyes, or maybe she thought I should wear green because Mr. Lafferty liked green. The shawl to cover my head was a lighter bluish color, more the color of my eyes.

Mrs. Wilson brought a couple of hoes for the farmers to use. Piper's mom had even made a tent-like thing out of wooden spindles and nylon fabric. She'd tried to make it look like a house or a tent that was blown down by the storms in my story, and she taught Margaret and Lacey how to make it work so that the house collapsed. Mrs. Wilson also cautioned us about the short ladder behind the mountain and how at the end of the play, we were all supposed to be on the steps like we had followed the Prince right up the mountain.

Finally Mrs. Wilson blew her whistle. "Quiet, everyone. Take your places."

Piper's mom checked everyone's position and reminded them how important their facial expressions were in mime. Mrs. Walker was back again, volunteering her time to teach us sign language just for H, and she talked to us about body language. She was careful not to call it *sign language* so there was no chance of spoiling the surprise.

Piper's mom reminded us of our body language too. Then she said, "Let's roll."

Mrs. Wilson started reading the story just like last week and the week before. But today, with everybody in costumes and on their best behavior, it felt different. It was so good. All the parents and even the choir members clapped when it was over. I didn't know if Mrs. Wilson was so excited she wanted to do it again or if she thought we needed the rehearsal, but she wanted us to do a repeat, and we did. It was good again. Even Mrs. Walker bragged on our faces and body language.

After the second time through, Mrs. Wilson sent us all to change out of the costumes. While Mom and Grancie folded them and put them away, Mrs. Wilson had the choir rehearse "Go, Tell It on the Mountain." Then she turned to me.

"Julia, why don't you play your piano piece? And then we can practice your solo." She accompanied me while I sang, but I didn't sign the song. I was saving that for Sunday and Mr. Lafferty.

When I finished, I asked Mrs. Wilson if Piper could do

her dance for us. Piper didn't have her costume, but she was always ready to dance. She surprised her mom and wanted to start the dance from the top of the mountain. She said she could start from the stool Dad had built behind the mountain, and it would look like she was flying through the air when she came down. Her mom went behind the prop and studied it. She gave Piper the thumbs-up sign and turned on the recording from the boom box.

The song was about angels, and Piper told their story in her dance. When she danced, she even made me feel like I could dance, although I knew I couldn't.

"Okay, everyone. That was all marvelous. Just wonderful! And I know the performance itself will be just as good. Now, here are some important instructions about Sunday afternoon," she said as she handed out papers. "We'll be meeting here at the church at four thirty. Make sure you're not late, because we'll have to get costumes on and get ready to go. And we'll finally be explaining where we're going!"

She was so proud of how everyone had done in rehearsal, she didn't just give us M&M's from the bowl on the piano. She gave every one of us a whole bag of M&M's.

The rest of the week was busier than usual at the Russell house. The phone rang constantly. There was a flurry of activity—Grancie and G-Pa coming and going, sweet smells of vanilla and chocolate floating through the house, and Christmas music playing all the time. Mom was getting ready for Sunday and for the arrival of Aunt Jane and all her family on Monday. They would be visiting us for almost a week.

All week, I'd had trouble going to sleep. I was too excited. I practiced my song and my signs several times every night. And just before I went to sleep, I prayed. I prayed for everybody to stay well and to remember what they were to do. And I prayed hard that Mr. Lafferty would like it all.

Sunday afternoon, December twenty-third, finally came. We loaded the car and headed to the church. Everybody was chattering and trying to figure out the surprise of where they'd be going. The choir room looked and sounded like the Sycamore Hills Tigers had just won their homecoming football game until Mrs. Wilson blew the whistle. Even the parents knew what that meant. They lined up along the back wall, and the choir took their seats. Mom and Grancie gave us our costumes, and we put them on right where we were.

Then Mrs. Wilson stood in front of everybody. "Well, ladies and gentlemen, we've been waiting for this day for more than a month. You children have worked hard, and so many of you have participated in getting us ready for a performance you won't forget. If we had a drummer, I'd ask for a drumroll before I tell you where we're headed."

We didn't need a drummer. I started stomping my feet, and others began to join in, and before long we had our own drumroll right there in the choir room.

Then Mrs. Wilson said, "I can't keep it in any longer. I know because I was born in this town that we've all wondered about the green mansion out on the hill on the edge of town. That's where we're going today. There's a wonderful man who lives there, and we're taking Christmas to his house."

Everyone in the room was as silent and still as H and I had been the day the cardinals fed from my hands. They were shocked. Nobody had guessed that. Then one by one they started clapping. Mrs. Wilson asked Dad to come and explain.

Dad stepped out front. "Yes. Some of you may have heard how decades ago the people who built Emerald Crest had Christmas parties and invited practically the whole town. And now Mr. and Mrs. Lafferty and their daughter, Mackenzie, are in heaven. But their grandson lives at Emerald Crest. He is a brilliant and kind man who has never been able to hear. He uses sign language, and that's why Julia wanted to do the play in mime and have you sign the song you'll be singing. This party is to bring a little joy to Mr. Lafferty. So, with that, let's go. Follow me."

It didn't take long to load up. Dad drove out of the parking lot and led the caravan through town and across Cedar Gulch Bridge. We must have looked like a funeral procession. There it was, that green granite mansion on the hill, nestled between tall cedars all dressed in twinkling lights. At that distance, they could have been stars. Mr. Hornsby had made sure it was beautiful.

I could hardly wait.

It took forever to get up that hill. But finally, the cars all pulled up and lined the circular drive. We took care to get out of the vehicles and form up as planned. All fifty-four of us carried something as we approached the door.

Dad had called Mrs. Schumacher when we came through the gate. She made certain H was in the library out of sight of the car lights coming up the hill. She told Dad he was in front of his computer.

Dad wore his green sweater and red Santa's hat. I was next to him, and Pastor Franklin stood on the other side of me. I adjusted the napkin covering the contents of my basket and turned to see if Mr. Tinsley was behind me and ready with his fiddle. Dad rang the bell, not for Mrs. Schumacher, but so H would know someone was there.

Mrs. Schumacher greeted us and opened the door wide, and we entered in all our Christmas finery and costumes, singing and swinging baskets of home-baked goodies for the party we were about to have. I was so excited that my hands were sweating through my wool gloves. There hadn't been a Christmas party here in decades. And now this would be a glorious celebration just like H's grandmother used to have.

But then I saw Mr. Lafferty's wheelchair scurrying across the hallway in front of us. Without even looking, he darted into the elevator and disappeared. I was horrified. Maybe my idea hadn't been such a good one after all. Maybe I should have listened to Dad when he told me Mr. Lafferty didn't take to folks very well. Just thinking that, all the butterflies of excitement flew right out of my mouth.

The people kept pouring in, though, and Mrs. Schumacher steered them to the great living room, where folks emptied their baskets of holiday cookies and candy and other goodies on the tables already set up. We'd come with the whole party, even the urns of hot cider and a whole stage production. But H wanted nothing to do with it.

I watched Dad and Mrs. Walker and the pastor talking and then turned away. I didn't even want to know what they were saying. I just wanted to run out the front door and down that hill all by myself. I was the cause of this, and H would never want me to come back.

I looked up. Mrs. Walker was headed straight for me. She took my hand and led me over to where Dad and the pastor were talking in front of the elevator. When I got there, Dad knelt down and said, "Okay, Julia. This is your party. You have to go up and give Mr. Lafferty a proper invitation."

Now I knew I wanted to run down that hill, even if it was through the woods in the dark. Maybe I could find a hole to fall into like Derrick had. "But I can't go up there, and I don't know what to say."

"Yes, you do, Julia."

"No, I don't. I can't talk to him. I don't think he likes me anymore."

Dad looked me straight in the eye. "Julia, just tell him what you told me when you came up with this idea, and then do what you do best: Ask him questions."

"But I can't. I can't sign well enough yet to tell him what I'm thinking."

I knew I had no choice when Dad pressed the elevator button. I hoped it was stuck and would never open, but it did. When the metal door slid to the side, Dad nudged me in, and the rest of our small group followed. When the door opened again, it was to a wide hallway with green walls and dark wooden floors with light streaks, probably where H's wheelchair had made tracks. I had never been upstairs before.

Mrs. Schumacher pointed to where there was light coming from underneath the door at the end of the hall. Wooden birds perched on tables lining the hallway—chickadees, cardinals, and even baby birds carved into a wooden nest. We got closer and closer to that door, and the whole time I thought about how I didn't know what in the world I would say to him. H was going to be so angry he might fire Dad and Mrs. Schumacher for being in on my surprise party, and he'd probably never help poor people or make our town better again, all because of my stupid idea. I hadn't meant to make him upset. I'd just thought it was time the town brought him a little Christmas.

When we reached the end of the hall, Mrs. Schumacher pressed a button on the door frame. Lights flickered underneath the door. She opened it and stepped in. I could see her signing something to H, but Mrs. Walker didn't tell us what she said. That meant it was a private conversation. My palms were sweating, and my heart beat really fast, like when I had to read my short story in front of the class and Robby was sitting right in front of me.

Mrs. Schumacher motioned for us to come inside. The room was the biggest bedroom I had ever seen—a huge four-poster bed, a desk, a fireplace between two windows, books everywhere like in the library, and more unfinished sculpted birds and wood shavings on a big table next to the window. Mr. Lafferty sat with his back to us, staring out the window, but there was nothing he could see out there because it was darker than Aunt Ninny's smokehouse at midnight. He just wouldn't look at us.

Dad pinched my ear and nudged me closer to Mr. Lafferty. Mrs. Walker was close beside me to be my voice. I was able to sign *Merry Christmas, Mr. Lafferty.*

He still didn't move.

"We brought you a Christmas party to your house." Mrs. Walker moved in front of him and signed for me.

Mr. Lafferty watched her, but his hands lay silent in his lap. Mrs. Walker looked at me, waiting for me to say something.

"Mr. Lafferty, we brought you a party. There are people downstairs with Christmas cookies and candy and hot chocolate, and there are children ready to perform for you. They're performing a play I wrote just for you."

His hands were still, but he turned, and his eyes were glued to me. If I didn't know before, I understood right then why the birds would come to him. He could be as still as one of those statues he carves.

Dad said I was good at asking questions, so I thought I'd give that a try. "Mr. Lafferty, what do you think about our Christmas party? Wouldn't you like to come downstairs?"

He looked like he wanted to speak, but he didn't move a muscle, not even his eyes.

"Now, Mr. Lafferty, my grandmother told me all about the Christmas parties your grandparents used to have here—the food and the music and how much fun everybody had. I thought since you liked to hear me play the piano, you would enjoy having a Christmas party." Mrs. Walker kept signing after I stopped speaking and then folded her hands together. I didn't know what she'd said to him after I quit talking, but that didn't work either.

Neither my invitation nor my question and not even my explanation worked. I thought I'd try what Mom used: shame. "Mr. Lafferty, I know you have manners. Your mama and your grandmother taught you good manners, and you always use them when I'm here. I think it's time you use your manners and come downstairs. You have guests."

The only muscles that man used were his eye muscles, moving his gaze from Mrs. Walker's hands to my face. I decided to out-stare or out-be-still him, but that didn't last long, just enough time to give me another idea. "Well, Mr. Lafferty, if you won't come downstairs, I'll do my part right here." I stood up straight just like Mrs. Wilson taught me. I shook my hands a bit, and then I started to sing my words and sign them at the same time.

> *What can I give Him, poor as I am?*
> *If I were a shepherd, I would bring a lamb.*

Even in the grayness of that room, I could see Mr. Lafferty's tear-filled eyes, and as I kept singing, he raised his hands and began to sign with me. He knew the Rosetti poem.

> *If I were a wise man, I would do my part;*
> *Yet what can I give Him?*
> *Give Him my heart.*

When I finished, H just looked at me. I didn't know what to do, so I signed *Come with me, please.*

He slowly raised his hands and responded. *Wait.* Then he disappeared out a door.

Mrs. Schumacher whispered, "I think things will be fine, Julia."

I so hoped she was right, but I was worried he had locked himself in the bathroom and was never coming out.

I needn't have worried. In just two minutes, he came rolling through his bedroom just like he had that afternoon of my visit when he felt the vibrations of the piano—like he was on the way to the finish line. He had on a different shirt, a solid green one, and his wooly gray hair was combed, and he had a plaid blanket across his lap. Before he took my hand, he signed *Merry Christmas. Let's go.* He held my hand all the way to the great living room.

When we came in, everyone clapped the way people who are deaf clap, holding their hands above their heads and shaking them. H responded with *Thank you* and joined their applause.

I led him to where we wanted him to be. No more sheets on the furniture, and there was a big Christmas tree in the corner, and there were presents underneath. Mrs. Schumacher and Mr. Hornsby had been working hard.

G-Pa and Mr. Tinsley had already put the prop at the end of the room, and the lid to the piano was raised to the highest. When everyone was in place, four of our choir members rang handbells—not like the chiming of the hour, but happy sounds. Those bell sounds just bounced around that great big room, and I watched H's eyes. I knew he felt something.

When the bells finished ringing, Mrs. Wilson announced our play for everyone, and Mrs. Walker interpreted for H. Then Mrs. Wilson began to read my script. I watched my friends do their very best. They used their faces, and they remembered everything they were supposed to do. And when all of us had made it up the steps to the High Mountain, the whole room broke out in applause. That room was like an echo chamber, and it was loud. Even H clapped like a hearing person.

Then Mrs. Wilson motioned for us to come down and take our places at the piano. She announced, "And now, our choir will sing 'Go, Tell It on the Mountain.' We chose this song because it's appropriate for the play. But the most important reason we're singing this song is because a little birdie told us it is Mr. Lafferty's favorite."

H clapped again. And when we began to sing and sign, he joined us. I never saw him smile so much. I motioned for him to come to the piano, and he did. I signed *This is for you.*

And I sat down and played my jazzy version of his favorite carol and then played "Joy to the World."

All the time I was doing that, Piper was putting on her angel costume. When she was ready, Mrs. Wilson announced it, and Piper's mom turned on the boom box. The music sounded like I imagined the music on the High Mountain would sound, and Piper floated off the top of that mountain in her white costume. She looked like she had wings. She danced from one side of the room to the other. She was beautiful. When she finished, and her arms were spread wide like the smile on her face, Mrs. Wilson just all of a sudden started singing "Gloria, in excelsis Deo" and everyone joined her. That was not in our plan, but it was just the right thing to do.

Mrs. Wilson turned to me. I knew it was time for me to sing. I shook my head. "I don't need to sing, Mrs. Wilson."

She looked puzzled. "But you have the special song, and you're going to sign it?"

"Yes, ma'am. It was a special gift for Mr. Lafferty, and I already sang it for him."

Then she motioned for my dad to come up and say a few words. Dad came by Mr. Lafferty and shook his hand. "First, I want to thank Mr. Henry Lafferty the Second for opening his home and his heart to us this evening. Sharing your beautiful house with us is quite a gift." He turned to Mrs. Wilson. "And thank you, Mrs. Wilson, for all your hard work to get the choir ready. And thanks to all of you who brought Christmas goodies and Christmas cheer tonight. And I'd say it's time for some of those goodies. But before that, I have one more person to thank." Dad looked at me. "I want to thank my daughter, Julia. This whole party was her idea. She has worked for weeks. She wanted this to be a very special evening for everyone, and especially for you, Mr. Lafferty." Everyone started clapping again, even H.

After that, everyone went for the refreshments. H was a little shy at first, but then he started communicating. He went to Mrs. Wilson and to every child and said *Thank you for coming and for learning some of my language.* And people came up to him and said very nice things. Mrs. Walker's hands were so busy that night, making sure Mr. Lafferty understood everything that was going on. She told us later how much it meant to him that others would try to learn his language.

As people left, H told them he hoped they would come back next year. I hoped that meant he was not planning to fire Dad and that I was still his friend.

We were the very last ones to leave. G-Pa and Dad had already loaded the mountain into the truck, and Grancie and Mom helped Mrs. Schumacher tidy up. I stayed with H, and we had a conversation on the computer about Christmas and the play and Piper and everything that had happened.

At last, I heard Dad's voice. "Time to go. We don't want to wear out our welcome."

My whole family stood at the front door saying our good-byes. I told H I would call him tomorrow.

He raised his hands to me. Every child in the whole wide world knew what that meant. He took my face in his hands and kissed me on each cheek, then he hugged me hard for the first time ever. I hugged him back.

Finally, I had taught H to hug.

Epilogue

Sixteen years after the first Christmas party, 2018

MY LIFE IS WHAT IT is because of a moment on an autumn afternoon in 2002 when I first met Henry Lafferty the Second. I often wonder how different it would be if I hadn't met H and watched his hands move and slipped into his garden room to play the piano with real ivory keys.

And who could forget that first Christmas party? H's life is different too, because that was a moment that changed the way the townspeople related to him.

I hear voices in the kitchen—Grancie and Mrs. Schumacher chattering away like they do every Christmas. "So another year of pound-cake cookies? Red sprinkles this year?" I ask.

Mrs. Schumacher, now eighty plus, shakes her head. "Oh, Julia, your grancie's pound-cake cookies need nothing to make them more delicious or more elegant."

"I agree. I know the party's being catered, Mrs. Schumacher, but I'm so grateful you two will carry on some of our Christmas-cookie traditions." I hug Mrs. Schumacher and kiss

Grancie on the cheek. "And Grancie, you'll get to see your annual Christmas-at-Emerald-Crest poem in print this afternoon. Mom's bringing the programs out after she finishes her volunteer work at the hospital. I need to check with Mr. Hornsby and Mrs. Finch about a surprise." I wink at Grancie and leave the kitchen.

I walk through the dining room and spy Mrs. Finch in the foyer in her bare feet, arranging fresh holly in a large crystal vase. "Oh, that's lovely, Mrs. Finch. Would you like a pair of warm socks? That marble floor must really be cold."

She immediately slides her feet into her red stilettos. "Of course this is lovely. I designed it to be lovely. And no. I have no need for socks." She refuses to look at me.

"Well, you are certainly doing a good job." I am grateful she's unaware of my eye-rolling. "I thought I should let you know that my dad and Jackson will be arriving in a few minutes with a rather large prop that will be placed in the north end of the great hall."

"I do hope it's not some unattractive monstrosity."

"Oh, I can assure you that it is, but a necessary and memorable monstrosity. Now I should alert Mr. Hornsby. He can hardly wait for its arrival." I try hard not to grin.

Mr. Hornsby and his wife are empty-nesters now, and they live in the cottage H had built for them next to his studio. Mr. Hornsby knows every inch of this property, and he would die protecting H or Mrs. Schumacher. I see him headed to the studio and open the door to the garden.

"Afternoon, Mr. Hornsby. Just wanted you to know that Jackson and Dad are moving a mountain this afternoon. I can't believe that Dad found that thing he and G-Pa built sixteen years ago for our very first play. Found it among some rubble in the back of the shed. Remember that one?"

"Oh, I remember that mountain where the King lived. I helped them move it the first time, and I'm here to help today."

"Piper will be here to dance again. I don't care how she

dances on Broadway, it won't be more beautiful than seeing her float down from the top of that mountain in the great hall."

"Like an angel she was. So, your brother's coming?"

"Yes, sir. Jackson can write his sports column from anywhere, so he and Linda and the two boys will be here for several days. I'm the world's best aunt, you know."

"Yessiree. You just have a way with children, Julia. Gotta go—I hear a car out front. Probably Derrick. He's coming out to do a final walk-through of the building."

"Great. I'll speak with him when he finishes."

That's another life-changing moment—the moment when Derrick broke H's window and fell into the cave. He's never forgotten H's kindness in taking care of medical bills and his education, and now he is the architect and designer of all the new buildings at Emerald Crest. And today he's doing a final walk-through of Cardinal Crest, a boarding school where in just a few weeks we will open our doors to students who are deaf.

Our Christmas gala for the grand opening is day after tomorrow, and the staff is ready for the twenty-eight children who will be arriving in January.

H is seventy-six now, and he's still carving birds, reading, and expanding his world, and now he will be formally teaching. He will be our very best teacher. I say that with years of experience as his student. Oh, he's still the town's benefactor, and he thinks it's all in secret. But the good people of Sycamore Hill know, and they allow him his privacy, except at Christmas.

Henry rubs on the last bit of stain, holds it up to the window, and smiles with satisfaction. He covers the piece with a towel and heads for the elevator. No time for fancy wrapping. He has made Julia wait long enough.

The elevator opens and when he looks up, there she is at the piano. He pauses, allowing his eyes to survey the room and

Julia. He wonders how many hours she has spent there since her first appearance at his door years ago, bursting into his life with her natural curiosity and so many questions. She has learned his language, sat with him in the garden, carved birds in the shop, and visited the gravesites of his family. Julia couldn't bring sound, but oh how much music and life and companionship she has brought to him.

The warm memories spill from his heart as he sees her now, a beautiful young woman who has become the daughter he never had. Because of her he will have a legacy.

He sees her head turn toward him, those once bouncy blonde curls tamer now, but the same searching blue eyes, and always that impish smile.

I sit at the piano and do what I often do here, but I hear the elevator. That means H is finished and I finally get to see it—my early Christmas present. Something covered in a mahogany-stained towel is perched in his lap as he rolls into the room and approaches the piano. He raises his eyebrows and then looks at the object. I sign *It's finished?*

H smiles and hands it to me. This work of art is worthy of a gold satin cloth and a public unveiling in the finest of galleries, but this is another moment—just mine and H's. I hold it at eye level and drop the stained towel to the floor, revealing a hand-carved, hand-rubbed pair of cardinals. It's not like the one cardinal ornament he has carved for me for the last sixteen Christmases. I am surprised but not disappointed. A pair of cardinals, one male carved with perfection, and a juvenile female sitting on the limb next to him, looking up at the male. It's a replica of the Cardinal Crest logo, and it will have a prominent place on my desk forever.

Our hug is a beautiful benediction for this moment.

H rolls away, and I move to the window overlooking the

garden, and my memories shower me like that blanket of snow that covered Emerald Crest sixteen Christmases ago. That December night was the beginning of a friendship that directed my life in so many ways. Grancie always told me about moments, but with H, I learned the importance and the sacredness of the moment when two human beings connect in a deeply spiritual way—the way H and I did.

I watch the snow falling through the bare branches of the sycamore tree and remember many afternoons with H, learning his language and how to carve birds, and how H taught me to be patient, and how to be quiet, and how to think about words and language, and how to turn *can'ts* into *cans*. I think the only time we were separated was when I went off to Texas to college so that I could get a degree in deaf studies and then stayed to get my law degree.

I am now the Russell family's next generation attorney, and I'll be here to take care of H and to run Cardinal Crest as executive director and teacher. I manage to get to Washington, DC, frequently, where I am an advocate for people who cannot hear and who need a voice.

I move my hand to my necklace, remembering when H lifted the lid of the box that held the first Christmas gift I gave him. I still can see his round little eyes filled with tears as he pulled that red and green lap quilt from the box. I fully expect him to get it out again this Christmas as he has done every Christmas since I gave it to him.

Sometimes I look around these halls and rooms and out these framed windows, and I wonder about the life-changing moments that have happened here. I twirl the chain of my necklace around my left index finger, and I see my twelve-year-old self opening my birthday present from H—a special gift that I rarely remove. The necklace that was his mother's, with a small emerald set in a gold heart.

I run my right hand over the smooth wings of the hand-carved cardinals. H has given me so much, but his greatest gift

to me is himself. Rich are the memories I have of the silent days
I spent with him. Most of all that one holy night in December
so long ago.

Acknowledgments

As always, I begin by acknowledging you, the reader. More than likely, you're reading this during the Christmas season, perhaps the busiest time of the year. Yet you made a choice to spend some of your hours with this book. Thank you. My hope is that it was worth your time. Maybe for you, reading this book was an escape, or a reminder of some truth, or just a few hours of relaxation to get you in the mood for Christmas. If it has enriched this Christmas season for you in some way, then I am a most happy writer.

You've heard it takes a village. It does. The team at Gilead Publishing is the best. Thank you, Becky Philpott, Jane Strong, Jordan Smith, and Katelyn S. Bolds for all the work you do behind the scenes that puts this book in the hands of the reader. You're so responsive, and you're bold with creative ideas and answers.

Every author dreams of an editor like Leslie Peterson—one who knows her commas and colons and makes suggestions with delicate compassion. Thank you, Leslie, for asking all the right questions and for your precision and patience. You're the best.

I'm so grateful for friends and family who do not abandon me because I need solitude to write. You do know you're the source of many ideas, don't you?

As always, I am so grateful for my Bill. He makes living easy when I'm working. He's always there when I ask, "What do you think about … ?" And then his biggest encouragement is the way he eagerly awaits when I emerge at the end of the day and he wants me to read to him the next installment.

And there is my heavenly Father, the Author of life, stepping down out of His heaven and bringing us Christmas. How grateful I am You came. Your coming changed history, and Your coming changed my life story. Thank you, Father, that because of You, all our stories can have a happy ending.

Grancie's Pound-Cake Cookies

This recipe is so easy, and the ingredients are ones we always have on hand. It's a great little buttery cookie like Grandma used to make. Enjoy!

Ingredients

1 cup (2 sticks) butter, softened (Don't even think about a substitute.)

1 cup sugar

2 egg yolks

1 teaspoon vanilla extract (I also like ½ teaspoon vanilla and ½ teaspoon almond extract.)

2 ½ cups all-purpose flour

Instructions

Preheat the oven to 350 degrees F.

In a large bowl, cream the butter and sugar. Stir in the egg yolks. Add in the vanilla and flour and mix until combined.

Taking about a heaping tablespoon of dough into your hand, roll it into a ball and place it on an ungreased cookie sheet or one lined with parchment paper. Flatten it with a fork to about 1 ½ inches in diameter. Repeat with the remaining dough.

Bake in a 350-degree oven until the edges are brown, about 10 minutes.

Makes 3 to 4 dozen cookies.

Variations

Sometimes I use this recipe as a base with another ingredient to make a variation on this cookie. Try these—just one at a time, please.

- ½ cup chopped pecans
- ½ cup coconut
- ⅓ cup maraschino cherries, drained and chopped (I decorate the top of this cookie variation with ½ of a cherry.)
- Sprinkles (Before baking, brush the top of the cookie lightly with milk so the sprinkles stick. Doing this over a large sheet of wax paper makes for easy clean-up.)
- Chocolate ganache (Drizzle over the top of the cookie. Again, wax paper is a work saver.)

Grancie's Iced Pumpkin Cookies

This morsel of goodness is a soft and moist cookie that begs for a cup of tea on a fall afternoon. Or really any time. A couple of these in a snack bag make delicious Halloween treats too. Oh, and they smell so good!

Ingredients

2 cups sugar

2 cups (4 sticks) butter, softened (That's right, 4 sticks!)

1 16-ounce can pumpkin puree

2 eggs

2 teaspoons vanilla extract

4 cups all-purpose flour

2 teaspoons baking powder

1 teaspoon baking soda

1 teaspoon salt

2 teaspoons ground cinnamon

1 teaspoon ground nutmeg

½ teaspoon allspice

2 cups raisins

1 cup chopped pecans or walnuts

1 cup powdered sugar

Milk

Instructions

Preheat oven to 350 degrees F. Grease a large cookie sheet (or line with parchment paper).

In a large bowl, cream the sugar and butter until fluffy. Add the pumpkin, eggs, and vanilla extract and blend well.

In another large bowl, sift together the flour, baking powder, baking soda, salt, cinnamon, nutmeg, and allspice.

Slowly add the dry ingredients to the creamed mixture and blend well. Stir in the raisins and nuts.

Drop the dough by tablespoonful 2 inches apart onto the cookie sheet. Bake in a 350-degree oven until lightly browned, about 12 to 15 minutes.

Place the cookies on a rack to cool before glazing.

Glazing

In a small bowl, combine the powdered sugar with the milk one teaspoon at a time until the sugar is the consistency to spread easily with a knife. If the glaze is too thin, add more sugar. If too thick, add milk just drops at a time.

Place the cookies on sheets of wax paper (it makes for a much easier clean-up). Use a spoon to drizzle the glaze on the tops, then the back of the spoon to smear the glaze enough to cover the top of the cookie. Allow the glaze to harden, then place the cookies in an airtight container for storage.

Makes approximately 5 dozen cookies.

About the Author

Phyllis Clark Nichols's character-driven Southern fiction explores profound human questions using the imagined residents of small town communities you just know you've visited before. With a strong faith and a love for nature, art, music, and ordinary people, she tells redemptive tales of loss and recovery, estrangement and connection, longing and fulfillment ... often through surprisingly serendipitous events.

Phyllis grew up in the deep shade of magnolia trees in South Georgia. Born during a hurricane, she is no stranger to the winds of change: In addition to her life as a novelist, Phyllis is a seminary graduate, concert pianist, and cofounder of a national cable network with health- and disability-related programming. Regardless of the role she's playing, Phyllis brings creativity and compelling storytelling.

She frequently appears at conventions, conferences, civic groups, and churches, performing half-hour musical monologues that express her faith, joy, and thoughts about life—all with the homespun humor and gentility of a true Southern woman.

Phyllis currently serves on several nonprofit boards. She lives in the Texas Hill Country with her portrait-artist husband.

Website: www.phyllisclarknichols.com
Facebook: facebook.com/PhyllisCNichols
Twitter: @PhyllisCNichols